T0062996

Angel Heart

Gypsy Lee Rose

BALBOA.
PRESS

A DIVISION OF HAY HOUSE

Balboa Press books may be ordered through booksellers or by contacting:

Balboa Press
A Division of Hay House
1663 Liberty Drive
Bloomington, IN 47403
www.balboapress.com.au
1 (877) 407-4847

Print information available on the last page.

ISBN: 978-1-4525-2948-6 (sc)
ISBN: 978-1-4525-2949-3 (e)

Balboa Press rev. date: 06/23/2015

Contents

I would like to thank my husband for inspiring me and giving me the confidence to write this book and to keep me going during the tough times when I almost didn't think I would complete it to the end. A special thanks to all my family and friends that have helped with ideas and support during these hard past five months. And finally thanks to the Publishers for taking a chance on me in the first place. It has now opened the doors and my confidence to get started on my next book.

Gypsy Lee Rose

1

Summer Romance

It was January the tenth 2011, and Angel Hart and Jett were both back to their respective jobs after four weeks of annual leave for the Christmas festive break. Although it's clear Angel definitely wasn't in work mode, Jett was hard at it back at the forefront of Hunter's Construction site which was the newest and latest building site of "The Mega Plaza". A modern day shopping hub which is too include over a hundred specialty shops and department stores, grocery and retail outlets an electrical and / hi fi store, post office, newsagency, pharmacy and a local medical practice. It will also host an eight cinema movie theatre.

Angel was daydreaming and gazing out the window, thinking about the sexual rendezvous she had been having over her summer holiday break. Thinking about the past weeks was already making Angel very wet and horny. She could feel the moist knickers from her sex where her sexual feelings had become so intense she thought she was going to orgasm on the chair she was sitting on.

Never in Angels wildest dreams did she think she could ever get so hot and horny and wanting and needing more sexual gratification since her first encounter with Zane Channing.

He did something to her! He ignited a passion deep inside of her. A new door had opened her to a world of sexual deviation and depravity.

Clock watching for that anticipated hour when the time reached four thirty pm, Angels knock off time. It had been a long day for Angel after four weeks annual leave from her job as Manager at Fergusson's, Accounting Company.

Angel had started at Fergusson's at the tender age of 17, where she was offered an internship straight from school after completing her HSC.

Eleven years later and Angel had been promoted to Manager of finance and accounts.

A job Angel takes not only very seriously but with great pride, joy and gusto. She's worked hard to gain a position in a mainly male dominant role. May I add she is very proud of her accomplishments to date?

Angel's desk was piled high with contracts and past due work schedules that needed her attention.

Her mind though was subdued of the work load they lay in front of her.

Angel's only thought process was focused on her holiday romance, which had her daydreaming about the events that had occurred over the festive season.

Just as Angel was preparing to pack up for the day she was buzzed by Wade Fergusson, owner and Executive Director of Fergusson's Accounting, and her boss, who started the company some thirty years ago.

Angel have you got the Carter Contract completed and ready for me to finalise and sign of. I'm meeting with Jason Carter for dinner tonight to close the deal. I can't afford to lose this deal.

Angel this Deal is a real ballbreaker for this company! It's also worth a significant pay rise for you as well.

Yes Wade! "Angel replied". I'll bring it in right now

Thank you!!. And can you please cancel all my appointments for tomorrow? I'm meeting with a new potential client.

Consider it done Wade and I'll see you on Wednesday morning.

You most definitely will Angel bright and early we have a lot of work to catch up on.

I'll be here with bells on. Bye and have a good evening!

Angel watched the clock minute by minute. Finally the clock hits 4.30, Angel grabs her bag and mobile phone and races out the door, wasting no time getting out the building and to the car park where her prized BMW convertible is waiting in her car park.

"Thank fuck the fucking day is over says Angel" I couldn't have stood another minute in the blasted office today. Now home to shower and dress and off to the club.

Angel's mind is still focused elsewhere! Showered and changed Angel's nerves are shot to pieces with the sexual connotations and thoughts of her sexual escapades with none other than Zane Channing.

Driving in the BMW she's still daydreaming. Hoping Zane will be at the club and take her home and make hard, steaming, long, passionate love to her. The same erotic bad arse, sensual sex. That made her so wet and needing more and more to try to feed her sexual appetite of lust. Zane had opened her eyes to a new wave of hard-core pornographic lewd, fulfilling sexual frenzy.

This was all Angel could think about. Never in all her sexual experience had had she ever endured anything like the sexual journey of sexual debauchery that Zane had introduced her to?

The wild frenzied attack he made on her body, the way his tongue and mouth lingered over her entire body. He sucked and pulled at her taut nipples until she was writhing and screaming. She didn't know if it was pleasure or pain. All she knew was that she kept praying and begging for more. Don't stop Zane! Let's stay here for ever! Don't leave me. No one else can make me feel the way you do. No sexual partner or lover has ever driven me to the depths of despair and made me that horny that my vulva is swelling to bursting point and my fleshy lips are raw and wet with lust and need from the fucking I've endured by the mercy of your big thick rigid cock pounding in my pussy so hard it feels like its bursting through the other side and out my anus. The way you suck my pussy dry with your tongue and eat at my anus like there's no tomorrow. Your tongue in my anus drives me wild and then you eat out my pussy like a hungry bear cub with your fingers in my arsehole I become paralysed and motionless. The climax is so extreme that sweat and heat pour out of me. I'm writhing and moaning, my body can't take any more I try to move you off me, only to have you penetrate deeper and harder inside my tight, wet pussy. My hands tied to the bed rails I'm still shaking, screaming moaning while you're pounding my pussy so hard that I feel some of your pre cum it's enough to keep me moist and to keep you fucking me into another world. I'm bursting, fulfilled exhausted. Your expression is one of euphoric, satisfaction, gratification, hunger. Your climax is building inside you! I'm begging and pleading you to stop. You slow down the strokes pulling and pushing it in out slowly making me pay for being such a bad girl. Finally you're pumping us to exploding point. I see the look on your face, the look of strain, satisfaction, pleasure, and fulfilment your own orgasm building. I feel the bursting and jerking of your cock, ejaculating into my very sensitive well fucked sex.

After their sexual encounter they lay in each other's arms. Angel lays with Zane's limp sticky cock in her hands as they both ponder and wonder, trying to come to terms with the realisation of what just happened between them each time more intense, than last time, more pleasurable, and more explosive and powering than before.

Angel stop being ridiculous! You're dreaming. Why would he want to have a romance with me? What do I have to offer the Dynamite himself?

My minds telling me to forget about the raunchy sexual romance her and Zane had enjoyed over the holidays. It's over now!

Mr Dynamite has probably moved on with his new conquest/s (lucky bitch) whoever she may be? She snarls!

But her hearts telling her that she is wrong about Zane, that he will turn up at Night Lights and be just as anxious and aroused for her as she is for him?

Angel's hoping he's going to be waiting, for her so they can rekindle where they left off, just the week before.

Seven o'clock on the dot Angel arrives at Night Light's Club, full of hope and optimism that this steamy hot lover is there to greet her. Just the thought of this already makes Angel so wet and moist. She is so wet she could wring the wetness out of her panties. "Geez" how could one guy have this effect on me? She has never felt like this before.

Zane has consumed all her thought processes, she can't think about anything else or doing anything else. Her mind just takes her back to her steamy romance with the most gorgeous sexiest, hottest most sensual perverted lover she has ever been with, he taught her things she only ever dreamt about or read in books. Never for one moment did she think this could possibly happen to her? But it did and now she can't get enough. The yearning and want in her body leaves her with an ache that cannot be satisfied. Not even her vibrator can replace the hands, mouth and cock of one Mr Dynamite Zane Channing.

Angel is greeted by long-time friend and co business partner Braxton Miles. They grew up together in the northern Sydney suburb of North Shore, where they went to school together and did everything together. They shared the same interests, the same friends, the same goals and even graduated from high school together along with Angel's twin brother Jett.

Angel set her goals in owning and operating her own business and Braxton was only focused on becoming rich. A great combination in the making, they both worked extremely hard to get some money behind them. They bought a cheap establishment decked it out and turned into an ultra-modern new age night club. This was the start of Night Lights club. An over eighteen's club and bar where the best drinks were served the best bands and music played and the best damn service in Auburn Creek was made available to the public.

But Night Lights holds a deep secret that is only known to selected people that meet a special criteria and a special selection process, and is kept out of the radar and from public view.

Angel Hart is a buxom honey blonde beauty with a petite 160cm frame with beautiful sea blue eyes and a perfectly tanned body of a golden sand colour.

Angel Hart is the local part owner of Auburn Creek's only adult only bar and night club Night Nights which she is in partnership with her long-time friend and business partner Braxton Miles.

Although at work and in public Angel holds herself with much grace and confidence, a self-proud business woman who has had to work extra hard to maintain the role usually held by the more masculine, dominant male in this cut throat male dominated world of accounting has found and made her niche in the engorged world of testosterone filled male gender.

Angel has a twin brother Jett Hart who heads up the role of Foreman in their local Construction Company Hunters Building and Construction. Jett started his apprenticeship with them when he also turned seventeen, and five years later he now heads up the company. Jett took over the reins of Hunters Construction's from founder and owner William Hunter who happily retired more than three years ago to enjoy quality time with his wife of more than forty years, their children and their grandchildren. This role couldn't come soon enough, for William. On William's retirement he handed over the reins of the company and ownership to Jett.

Growing up Angel and Jett were inseparable. They did everything together and although Jett older by only one minute has always been Angels protective older brother and her best friend. Jett, Angel and Braxton were known as the three musketeers.

They fled from their family life as soon as they left school at seventeen.

"Never, to return, home again". "Never any regrets"

Their new life in Auburn Creek was always shrouded with mystery among the locals, who often wondered why three teenagers alone without family had set up home and made new lives for themselves in quiet old country Auburn Creek.

What or who are they running and hiding from? That question is always on the locals minds.

2

Night Lights

ngel is greeted at Night Lights by her long-time friend and co business partner Braxton Miles.

"Hi Miles how's it ticking tonight"?

"Actually Angel it's pretty fucking heavy tonight?" Full on masses of crowds rolled in early tonight and we have even picked up some newies tonight too!

"Awesome! That's really great Braxton it's just what we need."

I can cover for you now if you like for you to go on your break?

"Thanks Angel that would be great!"

"Braxton has anyone asked for me tonight?" "No why?" Like who?"

"Oh nothing I was just wondering?"

Braxton could see the look of disappointment on Angel's face! But for the life of him he didn't know why?

"Move on Angel and forget about Zane". It was only a holiday romance after all. He never promised you anything of him. "Anyhow what would he see in someone like me?" why would he want to be locked into a permanent relationship with me? "What could I possibly offer "Mr Dynamite" himself? I bet he has women everywhere falling at his feet! He certainly doesn't need me. But fuck I sure as hell need him or at least need what he does to me and how he makes me feel.

Night Lights is a modern outlook on adult night clubs that has all the action of a normal nightclub but with a twist.

In a special warehouse at the back of the club is by invitation or request only "Sex Club". It makes way for the people that want to take sex acts to a whole extreme new level and reach new heights, the sexual deviates, the clients who like swinging, anal, S and M, dominance bondage, male to male, orgies, play acting kinky sex, who have fetishes who want them played out or just those that want that bit of something else that is just that bit inhibited and different.

Night Light's was the brainstorm of Angel Hart's best friend Braxton Miles. Both of them had plans growing up as children to own their own businesses that would thrive and pay their way through life for both of them. Their dreams started as children, progressed in their teens and they made it happen in adulthood. Their passion for business never changed.

Braxton and Angel started working after school and on weekends from the age of fourteen years to save for their future endeavour.

Angel worked in a retail department store and Braxton at a McDonald's fast food chain. Both of them picked up as many extra shifts as possible and worked all their school holidays. They saved and banked every hard earned dollar they made. Missing out on all the things the young ones of their generation wanted such things as Ipods, Ipads, laptops, fashionable clothes and shoes and mostly the choice to go out and have fun, mix with friend and enjoy themselves.

Both Angel and Braxton made the hard choice at the start to sacrifice all of these things for the one thing that meant the most to them, very own business venture.

Over the next five years they all three musketeers graduated together and all were offered very good jobs with substantial pay packets.

Braxton and Angel's bank accounts looked very good with both of them having substantial deposits.

Together they both decided it was time to find a financial lender who was willing to finance their much hoped for venture.

One bank in particular was so impressed with their savings, their sheer determination, and the aspirations that he agreed to finance the loan if they found the right property and the right location that would ensure the bank that they could adequately service the loan.

Every spare moment between their working hours they were searching adverts, the internet and driving around suburbs and outer regions in search of their ideal building that would become their dream business a night club.

After a year of searching Angel and Braxton struck gold when one of the agents that they were dealing with called them one Monday afternoon in November and told them that a double space had come up for sale.

The Agents name was Robert Willard. He explained to them that it used to be an old pub which housed its own brewery at the back and that this would be a great place for their new business and even better a high end return investment. Robert also explained to them that it used to be a family owned and operated business but both the parents passed away, the sister was married and living overseas and the brother who was in charge of the sale was consumed by his own business interests and that he could not run them all so decided it was a waste of his time, which only left one decision. To sell the business!

Braxton and Angel were so ecstatic and bursting with joy that they asked Robert if they could go straight down to the allotment have a look at it and possibly if everything was ok they would put a contract in to purchase the property.

Robert agreed to meet them both at five thirty pm. The property is called "Cowboy Joe's" and is on the Southern outskirts of Auburn Creek. The address is 111 ST. Albans Valley Rd. Auburn Creek.

With the greatest excitement and anticipation Braxton and Angel jumped in Braxton's 4x4 Toyota four wheeler and they drove to the destination. As expected Robert was there to greet them.

Robert unlocked the premises and led the way around the two buildings. The first building at the front was just as Robert had explained.

Angel's eyes were fixated on the structure and the potential this business had to offer.

Braxton also had an eye for details and was foreseeing exactly the way they wanted to fix this place up their way. They both had a vision and an insight of what was yet to come. Both were overjoyed even though neither had even seen the warehouse out the back as yet!

Robert led the way through the pub backdoor. There was a fairly long walk down a path to the warehouse which was separated from the pub. It was absolutely enormous; it had finely etched architraves and mouldings around ceilings, windows and doors. Chocolate brown walls which made the building look very dark and uninviting and it truly did smell just like a brewery.

Angel although not as excited and enthusiastic about the warehouse as she was the pub could still see the potential that could be made with the right renovations, brighter colour schemes and some soft touches. "Braxton agreed". Angel this is all just so perfect, so surreal, Angel wake me and please tell me this is not a dream.

"Braxton"! "Yes he replied to Angel?" I love everything about these properties, I love the character and charm of the old Heritage look, and the age of the buildings and most of all I think it's the best damn location in all of Auburn Creek. "Agreed said Braxton" and I think our new partnership starts right here! "I guess as a package we can always use the warehouse for our stock and storage." "No forget it Angel I have much bigger plans for our warehouse for which I want to discuss later with you about my thoughts! Believe me Angel you will be shocked, but I believe that we really are on a winner with our new venture and not to underestimate not only its worth but the potential growth we can forecast to bring us in."

"Ok Braxton you seem to know what we're doing, so why don't we sign the contracts as soon as possible, pay our deposit, and then take the contracts to the bank to sign them?"

Great idea replied Robert and Braxton. They both agreed to meet Robert at his office at ten am sharp the next morning. By ten thirty the contracts were signed and their deposits paid. They both took their contracts to their bank manager who liked over them with a fine tooth comb, did the appraisals and twenty four hours later phoned them both with a big fat approval. "Congratulations to you both on your future venture. It has been a pleasure and such a rewarding experience to do business with two genuinely committed smart business minded people with a vision and a flair and with some actual knowledge in the business world. I can see this being a sure fire hit, and if I can ever help you in the future with any extra money or another loan please don't hesitate to contact me. It has been an honour to you both to serve you in the interest of my bank and the foreseeable profits I can see coming back to the bank."

No we need to thank you! Without you our dream could never have been possible so thanks again, and yes all our banking and future dealings will be coming directly to you. Here is to our future.

"Now open up the champagne god damn it Angel we have a celebration to cheer for." The four of them drank champagne and relished in their new found dream of success which will certainly become a reality in the very near future. Braxton and Angel both new the celebration was an understatement because their dreams and visions had suddenly become reality.

Driving home from the bank Angel told Braxton that they needed to put their heads together straight away and make some solid decisions as to the direction they wanted to take this club.

The name of the club they had already decided on years beforehand. Because people go night clubbing at night and it needs to be well lit up the club name was obvious, and that is how it became "Night Lights".

Now Braxton can you please tell me what your vision is for the warehouse because frankly at the present moment all I'm seeing is store room and stock room?

Ok! Angel I've been doing a lot of research and in this day and age people's needs and desires have changed. People have become more open to things that used to be labelled taboo, or it wasn't right to act out your ideal fantasy. Now it's a person own individual choice and given right to act out what people of today now call "the norm".

"Braxton what are you on about"? And just what are you trying to tell me?

"Angel we can turn the warehouse into an exclusive specialised "sex club"? For the people that want to explore their sexuality beyond what would be considered the norm. They can come here and act out their sexual fantasies, individualise what they find gets them off and not feel ashamed or misguided in believing that sex is all about the missionary position. They can come here as an open minded individual or they can be covered if they're not happy to be exposed for fear of repercussions or what others may think. They the individuals can come here and do whatever weird arse thing they might be into and know that there are not only others that like this kind of sex but that they can come here and not be condemned and ridiculed because how sex pleases them doesn't always work for other people.

This place can service the male to male, orgies, S and M, bondage, dominance, slavery, kinky sex and also clients with fetishes and ones who like to play act. Couples and groups often seek these places out because they find this kind of sex is often missing in their relationships, they haven't got an environment where they can act out their pleasures and then there are the ones who want to be able to openly express themselves through their own sexuality and act out whatever it is that turns them on. By coming here it enables to not feel isolated or ashamed and that they are here with others who have chosen alternative sexual lifestyles who can be free and not looked at like there some kind of predatorily deviate and frowned upon, sinned and outcast because they don't measure up to how society thinks sex should be used. It will be an exclusive club with exclusive clientele. No invitation or request no entry.

So Angel what do you think?

"Braxton I think you have lost your fucking marbles". How do you expect to get a license for this place may I dare ask?" Please pray tell how you expect to pull of this illegal establishment?

"You're so naïve Angel!" We're not applying for a license. It is specifically for the purpose of people who like to step into the world of sexual debauchery, who don't want sex in the old missionary position, who want to explore new adventures, act out sexual fantasies and feel no shame and who belong amongst a minority who have the same views and ideas on how they want their sex to be. We set the business up on line and believe me the kinds of clientele that use these establishments will know how to look to find our listing. They email us the required criteria we ask for and check their background and history and all the clients are fully screened, they have to produce a current medical certificate to show that they are clear of any STD's including Hepatitis A and C, AIDS and HIV.

Once all the criteria is met, there history and background checks are done and we have their current medical history, then we can go ahead give them a booking, tell them the address and upon their arrival we collect an entrance fee payment, if they have a room then they pay for the use of the facility. They will also pay a booking fee to cover some of our costs and if they want to purchase any of our merchandise including condoms then that is another profitable return on our money.

Our club will consist of an open sex arena, private rooms for the wishes of the more discreet, a pole for the avid dancer or who just wants to do the tease act. There will be an open bar with minimal seating, a peep show room, a pawn theatre room and two slavery, dominant rooms for the customers that liked to be tied up, handcuffed, and whipped and so on. The place will have tough nut bouncers set in place for the just in cases? And we will have topless waiters and waitresses to serve up to the hungry thirsty appetites of our customers.

"Braxton Miles I've known you all my life and you never once mentioned anything like this to me before". Why is this? Can you please explain to me how you how you know about places of this nature? Because by geez I sure am interested to know!

"Firstly Angel I've never really found the appropriate moment to tell you about my insatiable sexual appetite". Secondly I use these types of establishments frequently.

"Oh my Lord Braxton what on earth possesses you to use a pornographic workshop or whatever you want to call them?" I really don't understand your need. You are gorgeously handsome, your shoulders are brawn and they have all the bumps in the right places, your eyes are a beautiful sea green colour. Your hair is always immaculate, never having a single hair out of place except for the most subtle hint of a spike on the top of your head. Your tall, dark tanned and your physique is so perfect, you can have the choice of any woman you want." Why for fuck sake a sex club?

"It is for that reason!" Women want marriage, kids, commitment the little house with the white picket fence and most of all fidelity. For which none of these things I want for myself. None of the women I've dated want to act out their fantasies or to help me relieve myself of mine. I want more than just the blow job or hand job or straight missionary sex in a bed I want adventure, torture, pain, pleasure, bondage, S & M, and even on occasion's orgies. I want all of that and more, I need more. I have a very large sexual appetite and

I want and need variety without the commitment. That's why places like this exist for people such as me who can come here and not be afraid to open up their sexual urges and worry about feeling outcast and ostracised. This kind of sex has been around for years Angel but no one could speak about it let alone go out somewhere and do these things without feeling strange. There are so many of us out there. You would be surprised. Angel I guarantee the minute were listed on our website we will be packed out because people that enjoy that bit more no matter how weird it may seem to be to some people it is someone's else's turn on or their ideal fantasy. No one really knows me or my fetishes or what it is that really turns me on. These types of clubs can give me that because there are others out there hidden away that come here and let loose and want the same kinds of sex as me.

You and me Angel we can offer that to others here so they don't have to travel away or sneak around to get their rocks off.

Believe me Angel the clientele is out there! Angel we can not only adhere to and accommodate their needs we can also make a killing in profits at the same time. And the profits are endless. You trust me!

If you're worried about the locals then don't?

No one from the area will even know it's here unless their actually looking for what we will have on offer. So those people don't talk they keep that part of their lives a secret.

Come on Angel what do you say? Is it a yes? I guarantee to make this work and we will reap the rewards of high profit margins.

"Fucking Hell" I must be crazy to let you talk me into this but if you want to and think you can make this work then who am I to get in your way. I do have a couple of requests first though is that we find another name away from Night Lights and second we give all the building, construction and designing to Jett and all the work to his men. He can organise all his own manpower to do all the work. We both will choose the designs, furnishings and colour schemes. That way our business is kept strictly in house and no outsiders can cause trouble and start rumours that would not be a good start for a new business.

"Done "Angel I also have a name already picked out! "Knicker Box" What do you think?

"I can cope and live with that" It does have a certain ring to it.

Now all we have to do is call up Jett to draw up some designs. We both go shopping for our décor and accessories and then wallah! We will be open for business. I think also Braxton we need to organise an "Opening Night "party for when it's finished.

"That is most definitely a plan Angel I'm with you on that score and also Angel thanks and cheers to a long lasting partnership in friendship and business"

3

Fergusson Accounting

*W*ade Fergusson is a distinguished masculine man 180cm tall, aquamarine blue eyes that shone like stars, and blonde sandy colour hair. For a man hitting just a touch on fifty his physique was trim and taut and he abs of steel, his body built like a solid German army tank which came from years of hard regimented workouts pushing himself to the limits in running, jogging and weight lifting.

Wade runs ten kilometres every day and then follows on with two hours of solid gym and weights. On top of everything else he in his spare time spends time with his wife and family and likes to play a round or two of golf in between. (He's not a man he is a machine) Angel mumbles under her breath.

Wade was born to wealthy well to do parents, born and bred in Auburn Grove.

Jansen Fergusson, Wade's dad was a high powered lawyer who went on to be one of Sydney's most renowned Supreme Court Judges.

Charlotte, his mum was a long standing teacher and for the last twenty years before her retirement she became the principal at Auburn Grove Area School. When his parent's retired they moved and settled up on the North Shore of Sydney at their palatial beach estate.

Jansen Fergusson always had plans of Wade following in his father's footsteps and becoming a lawyer and then a judge like him.

Wade young, rich and rebellious had other ideas. Ever since the family could remember Wade was forever counting his money. Thus he found his niche working with numbers hence along came accounting. Wade would never spend any money; he saved every cent he earned. Whenever he would get money for birthdays, and Christmases he would never spend it. It would go into his bank account and nothing would ever provoke Wade to withdraw any money that was ever deposited. Wade set himself a goal to become a millionaire by the time he was thirty. He went to University got a degree in Accounting and was certified and practicing by age twenty three. With his savings and a very small low interest loan he bought and started Fergusson's accounting. The contracts piled in from all the locals and then stretched outside of Auburn Creek and within two years Fergusson's had already grown into a multi-million dollar company. It is now listed in Forbes as a company worth in the billions and employs over fifty staff.

Angel Hart left school at seventeen and with no job prospects, experience or direction she applied for an internship at Fergusson's and scored the job. Angel managed to work her way up the corporate ladder to her top current position of Finance Manager and Personal Assistant to Wade Fergusson.

Wade hands over a new account to deal with, Rogue Tyler who owns the local automotive sales, mechanics and spare parts shop in Auburn Creek. To the locals Rogue Tyler is the lovable larrikin who likes to lavish himself and his women in luxury.

Tyler is much known to the local club where you would find him every afternoon and evening drinking alcohol, romancing the women and gambling.

The locals think that butter wouldn't melt in his mouth, but for some reason Angel since being close to him and doing his books gets a UN easy feeling around him. Although she can't quite put her finger on why she feels this way, she tries her hardest to avoid him and put distance between herself and Rogue. Is it is womanising ways? The sexual innuendo's he puts out to Angel? Or there are a lot of discrepancies in his books? There appears to be more spending on Rogues behalf to his total earnings. Angel vows to be wary and stay out of Rogue Tyler's way but to keep a close eye on him all the same.

Angel knocks on Wade's door! "Have you got a minute Wade? I need to discuss something with you! "Sure come in Angel" What's up?

I have been going over Rogue Tyler's books and I can't help feeling there's some shady work going on there! "What makes you think that Angel?" "Well there is no cash flow, he has no money his business and accounts and credit cards are booked to the hilt" although he lavishes himself in new cars, he has extravagant antique furniture through his house and he loses big in gambling every night.

Rogue spends big at the club buying the top of the range drinks he eats exclusive meals and wines and dines women all the time like there is no tomorrow. His personal and business accounts both show negative balance with huge outstanding debts owed to creditors. How is this lifestyle possible he is living with no money? Where is his cash flow coming from?

"Well Angel keep digging and working on his accounts and do some research but be careful and discreet" If then you're still not happy then take your thoughts and run them past Storm Mason and have him look into and see if there is anything illegal going on?

Storm Mason is the local Police Sergeant, born into a family of police officers. His father, ex-Chief of Police Russell Mason, his grandfather Chief Sergeant Ronald Mason, and his younger brother senior constable Hunter Mason.

Storm is an admirable man who is always willing to put his life on the line in the call of duty. His aim is to keep crime down to at least the bare minimum in Auburn Grove and keep the peace in the town.

Auburn Grove is a relatively close knit community and generally a crime free town.

Could Rogue Tyler be about to change Auburn Grove as a crime free town, or is Angel simply reading more into her feelings about Rogue and overreacting. Is her spirituality working in her favour?

Will Storm get to the bottom of Rogue's inconspicuous financial dealings?

Is Rogue the lovable larrikin he portrays to be? Or is that just a farce that he thinks others cannot see? Certainly the locals think he is what he seems. Or is he building up a port of illegal crime?

Storm Mason is a sharp shooting clear witted guy who will stop at nothing to get to the bottom of bringing justice to the criminals and their criminal activities. He is an over protective cop who will stop at nothing to keep people safe and keep the crims of the street. Storm takes pride in his job and is someone who glories in keeping Auburn Creek safe and free of any criminal activity.

Angels shift comes to an end so she decides to drop into the Police station to speak with Storm Mason about her findings with Rogue Tyler's books.

"Hi Storm how you are?" "Good Angel and what about yourself?" what brings you here on this glorious afternoon?

"Can I please talk to you in private Storm?" there's something that keeps niggling at me and it's troubling me?

"Of course Angel come through to my office!" What's wrong Angel? What do you want to talk to me about?

"Well Storm Wade's picked up the accounts for Rogue Tyler's automotive and he's asked me to handle the account"

"Yes that's straight forward Angel so what is troubling you then?"

"You see Storm there is no money in any of his accounts, he's mortgaged his million dollar house to the hilt, and he has a very expensive car collection and exquisite and very expensive antique furniture and décor throughout his entire property. He drinks like a fish, gambles incessantly and splurges and romances his bevy of female beauties. Meanwhile he has creditors screaming out for him to pay up and his debts run a mile long. Nothing makes sense to me! His accounts don't match his lifestyle or add up.

"I see Angel can you get some photocopies of his books, bring me copies of creditor demand letters and I will do a complete background check on his past and present business acumen. I'll organise a phone tap on all his lines and put surveillance on him at all times to watch for any criminal activity he may be involved in."

Please though Angel lay low, don't let Rogue know you're on to him and don't put yourself in harm's way or jeopardise your life or career? I'll meet up with you regularly to keep you updated on any new evidence if it comes to hand, play along and keep cool. Don't arouse Rogues suspicions.

"Thanks Storm I knew I did the right thing by coming to see you and making you aware, and I promise to stay calm and out of harm's way"

"Bye Angel I will be in touch soon!"

"Goodbye Storm I will look forward to seeing what you come up with"

Over the next week Angel gathers all the required copies of Rogue's accounts, documents, creditor demands, and his personal wealth and assets. Angel has all the documents sealed in an envelope addressed attention Sergeant Storm Mason and has them couriered to the police station. Now all Angel has to do is continue on and wait trying to figure out the unending mess of his books and wait for word back from Storm.

Angel sets to work and does a lands title search and an Australian Taxation search. "Fuck shock horror"! Angel is in awe of what she has found out and now she knows she has really opened up a can of worms.

4

Knicker Box

The summer is coming to an end and the contractors are working strongly together in order to make Angel and Braxton's opening night deadline. Knicker Box is expected to open sometime in May or June.

Knicker Box has been divided into four sections. The first section is the open arena which has no closed off doors is strictly open at all times and is amassed with masses and masses of floor cushions soft latex type mattresses and loads of cushions with fancy velvet like fabric that have zippers so the cushion covers can be removed and washed after each session. The arena is by far the brightest of all the sections in the whole area. The colours are strong tones purples both dark and light, blues ranging from the softest to the darkest, pinks with just about every shade imaginable and greens again ranging from the softest to the darkest.

It has raised ceilings with hand carved cornices and elaborate hand carved marble rosettes. This gives it a heritage look with a modernised twist. From each rosette's falls exquisite multi length crystal pendants with the faintest hint of gold embossing around the entire edges. There are pearl white encased shades on the end of each pendulum.

When the lights are on dimmer, a wonderful rainbow, array of flashing light beams shine throughout the entire arena which is called the loft. This sets the scene for very raunchy sex orgies, the swinging couples or for the folk that wish to explore their sexuality through other individual partners.

On the main wall is a full colour projector screen that continuously plays pornographic movies from a rear projector which is controlled from the main security room where everything electrical, electronic or security based come together and computer monitored at all times. For security factors each section is set up with full range security cameras so everyone and anyone are monitored at any one time.

The second section is like a dark dungeon. To enter you have to go through solid metal doors that will be opened by the press of a buzzer which is also controlled from the security control room. Pressing the buzzer lets security know you are down there ready to play, finished and wanting to move onto another section or to leave in general. The dungeon also has a complete intercom system and individual cameras set up for the clientele that want to film their sessions. It also helps cover all the safety aspects of each individual using the club. The dungeon is "known as the room of Debauchery."

It is coloured in shades of black, dark greys and reds and the furnishings are also in extremely dark colours of the same three colour combinations. These colours represent power, strength, control, fire, heat and lust.

It houses metal chains attached to the hanging frames with adjustable wrist and ankle restraints bolted to the top of the chain restraints and to the floor. These are fitted for the clients that like bondage, S & M, and who just like to be tied up and handcuffed. It's commonly used in Dominatrix and slavery and for fun role playing.

The dungeon rooms are equipped with fully washable latex mattresses and each bed is dressed with red satin sheets, bed covers and red, black and grey cushions. One complete side of the wall contains wall to wall cupboards which houses everything from, whips, handcuffs, chains, costumes, stiletto heeled shoes, condoms in every brand make and colour you could imagine sex toys and lubricants. Anyone in the need for sadism and masochism, bondage, slavery, dominatrix or anything sexual along these lines will find and enjoy the dungeon. It has been equipped especially with this clientele in mind. "Knicker Box's motto is to demand and to deliver."

To be a consumer of Knicker Box you need to subscribe to an annual membership fee, plus an entrance fee every time you enter the club. This fee enables you to use any room in the club except the "Peep show room" for which is a metered room where you pat for at fifteen minute intervals of five, dollars, for every fifteen minutes.

The clientele comes from registrations of interest of the Knicker box on-line web site. All bookings are anonymous and all transactions are received via credit card transactions only. Before any clientele are given instructions and locations all clients go through a tough screening process first carried out by "Knicker Box's" own security team if something doesn't match up then they don't get clearance. This is put in play to not only protect the staff but also the clientele. The other criteria that must be met for membership is a full up dated police clearance and a current up to date medical certificate to rule out any sexually transmitted diseases including hepatitis B & C and the Aids virus.

The club will accommodate up to a hundred clients per night and runs and operates four nights per week from Thursday nights to Sunday nights.

To gain entry into "Knicker Box" you must enter a coded gate way through a blocked of alley way which is well hidden and set back from the path to Night Light's. It's is well hidden by trees and is in complete darkness from the outside. Each guest is given the entrance code (which is changed every night after the club has closed) which must be keyed into the keypad at the front of the entrance doors in order for the double steel doors to open. Once you're in and certified by your own each individual number registered to your membership. If the two numbers match you will gain entry into the club.

When you walk into the club there is a multi-curve style antique wooden bar to your left that is stocked with every alcoholic beverage you could ever imagine. There are tables to sit at, or for added comfort there is soft leather couches scattered around the club to sit on. Naked waiters and waitresses will come around and serve you drinks of your choice and light snacks if you're a bit peckish. The entrance and bar area have nude and explicit artwork hung up on gorgeous white satin walls and green and gold leaf patterned curtains hang up at the three large windows surrounding the front area and bar. The lighting is down lights controlled by dimmer switches to set the mood of the individual client which change with the mood, heat and sexual tension throughout the evening.

The bar is made of an intricately carved mahogany wood with exceptional detailed carvings. The splash back glass behind the bar shelves has a clear diamond tint glass that glows and glistens when the lights shining on the glass.

Angel and Braxton walk around Knicker Box with the construction Foreman and Angel's twin brother Jett and soon Angel feels the moisture from her sex filling up inside her g string panties. It isn't hard to see by look on Braxton's face and the bulge that is quite obvious in his trousers that Knicker box is already having an effect on him as he excuses himself (in Angel's mind) gone to relieve himself from the rising pressure that has built up in him. The club has made Braxton's dick as hard as rock and the need that's filling up inside of him has him stroking his thick deep veined cock with long hard strokes while clutching and playing with his balls at the same time. His balls are so full of cum that the pressure to release his load is building deep inside of him. All Braxton needs to do is think about the types of places that Knicker box has resurrected from where his fantasies have been acted out and just knowing that his own place will now harvest his fantasies is enough for Braxton to give himself just one more stroke to bring him to the edge of his orgasm. With that thought in mind Braxton explodes and releases his cum into the toilet and gets the satisfaction and relief he needed. He knows his project will fulfil his own fantasies and that of the clientele and he's proud of what he and Angel have built between them. The sweat and the sexual tension that built up for Braxton shows just how intense Knicker box is going to be and what it has to offer not only for him but for the clients also.

Meanwhile Angel is dripping with saturated moisture coming from her soaking wet pussy as she thinks back to her romantic summer rendezvous with the gorgeous "Mr Dynamite" sexy Zane Channing.

Zane took Angel to her greatest sexual achievement bringing her to orgasm and leaving her weak, wasted and tired but always wanting and needing more. "Angel mumbles to herself (oh my god the sexual pleasure and orgasms we could both experience here could be unending)" "Stop it Angel your being ridiculous" you have had no contact with him since your last sexual phenomenon that started before Christmas and finished New Year's Day. During their four weeks together they experienced a full twenty four hours of pure adulterated sexual explosions and climaxes filling each other's needs and reaching new heights of orgasms coming together after each sexual activity they shared together. Angel's tears fall from her eyes as she wonders if she will ever see Zane again. Will their connection ever bring them back into each other's arms and their beds again?

Braxton and Angel do a walk around Knicker Box to make sure everything is going to plan and completion is going to finish on time for "Opening night."

The Opening night is set for Friday June the First, 2013.

Nearing completion Angel tells Jett about the finishing touches and the big clean up after him and his crew have finished the design and construction work.

"Jett are you aware that opening night is on Friday First of June?"

"Yes and I give you my word sis that the boys and me will be well and truly done and I will be alongside you on opening night!"

"Thanks Jett I guess I'm stressing out a bit now and going into panic mode." "Stop worrying it will be done!" Sis, have you seen, or heard anything at all, of Zane?" "No nothing!" I'm beginning to think I was just another sexual encounter for him over the summer!"

"Somehow Angel I don't thinks so!" The chemistry between the two of you couldn't have been more real. He was as keen and into you as you was for him! "I hope your right brother, because I'm certainly not feeling it at the moment." "You know his job takes him away even for months at a time." I bet you he will be back in your arms and bed in no time at all.

5

Jett Marks

Jett is the foreman of the local construction company in Auburn Creek. Angel and Braxton gave him the contract for building and designing of Knicker Box. Jett like Angel is a perfectionist in his own right. He started an apprenticeship at Hunters Building and Construction at the age of seventeen. The age both him and Angel were when they fled their home in Sydney and settled in Auburn Creek along with their best mate Braxton Miles. After his apprenticeship he worked his way up as foreman and now owns and runs the company. The former owner William (Bill) Hunter as he likes to be called retired three years ago to care for his sick invalid wife Rosie. Not having any children of their own they soon took a shine to both Jett and Angel and Jett became the children to them they never had. At the event of Bill's retirement he handed over the whole ownership and running of the company. In the event of both Bill and Rosie's deaths the company will be left exclusively to Jett and their entire fortune, assets, money and property are to be divided between both Angel and Jett.

Angel and Jett's childhood was both rough, terrible and abusive which left them both volatile and at the mercy of their mad, drunken father and a drug addicted useless mother who could see no wrong in their father's eyes. Or who lived in fear and just said nothing. Just sat back and watched as the kids were abused and terrified at the hands of their ogre father. They both made a pact growing up that as soon as they turned sixteen they would make a run for it, change their names move away and never look back. After arriving in Auburn Creek and knowing no one they were taken under the wings of Mr and Mrs Hunter. They saved every penny they earned from doing odd jobs and working after school to help pay their way. The Hunters however would never take any money, from them. They also didn't expect anything from them in return except to accept their love and for both the kids to respect them. A small price in Jett and Angels eyes for everything they had done for them. Shortly after arriving in Auburn Creek Braxton also followed them. Braxton's life wasn't much better except he lost his mum to cancer at age eight and his father lost all interest in Braxton's life. Never supplying him with food, money or anything a child needs to survive. Braxton survived on handouts from the neighbourhood, the local charities and anything Angel and Jett could both sneak out to him. Every night after their parents would both fall asleep drunk they would sneak him into Jett's room to sleep in the bed with him so he had somewhere warm and cosy to sleep.

Jett not very tall in fact the same size as his sister has the body of a Greek god. The muscles on his arms are as high as Mount Everest, his skin is Mexican colour tanned to a luscious brown olive colour. His tanned skin is due to him always working outside and in summer with no shirt on at all. His hair colour is snow white and is eyes are a sky blue and as clear as a bright sunny day. He keeps his body taut and terrific by working out every day at the gym.

Jett has no shortage of women lusting over him and throwing themselves at him on an almost daily basis, but his heart is for the one and only Madison (Maddie) Carson who he met through her being Angel's best friend and confidant. Maddie watched out for and comforted Angel when she landed in Auburn Creek and they have been best friends ever since. When Maddie first laid eyes on Jett she definitely didn't like or care for Jett too much. She thought because he was so good looking he wouldn't want a serious relationship he was just out to play the field. Jett's egotistical arrogance didn't get Madison's attention or approval at all. Finally after three long drawn out years pursuing and romancing Maddie, Jett finally won her over. They have been together ever since. Jett cherishes the ground Maddie walks on and almost every day brings her home flowers, chocolates, or even sexy lingerie.

Women off the town swoon over Jett and his romantic gestures and they are envious of Madison. Their sexual appetite is one of greed, lust and need. Their sex drive can have them making love three to four times a day and for hours at a time. Maddie owns the local gym where she regimentally works out every day and runs every day. She is also the town's personal trainer. Although Maddie is continuously working out or running she tells everyone that the sex with Jett is better, more fulfilling and much harder than a session at the gym could ever give her.

Both their climatic orgasms can be heard by the neighbours.

Madison is petite but doesn't have the curves in the right places like Angel does. Maddie's body is thicker set; the body of an athlete would definitely describe her body look, but still a wow of a body. She has jet black hair and dark brown eyes. Unlike Angel and Jett's childhood Maddie was born into a very close knit well to do caring and loving family. Madison worked in Admin for a small company in Auburn Creek until her parent's brought her the local gym and she heads up the admin for Jett who convinced her to come run the office of Hunter's Construction. She has just past her five year anniversary working for Jett and their ninth year anniversary of going out together is only a matter of months away.

Jett through his hard work and strong savings ethic acquired a great parcel of land just off the Main Road in Auburn Creek which has a flowing creek running directly behind the property. Jett has started building his and Maddie's dream home with the intention of hoping to have their elaborate fairy-tale wedding Madison has always dreamt about in the superb grounds of their beautiful house. Jett can only work on it in between his day work because he is so flat out with jobs. Construction work in Auburn Creek is plentiful.

Two weeks have passed and Jett, Angel and Braxton take their final walk around the completed Knicker Box site. Jett as he promised Angel completed the entire construction two weeks prior to the expected completion date.

Braxton's cheeky grin is bigger than a Cheshire cat over genius brilliant business plan and Angel are ecstatic over her design and décor choices and polished finished look and Jett's cocky smugness over his and his team's exceptional building and construction work.

Braxton leads Angel and Jett into their office and they settle up payment to Jett for his work. "Okay guys I have a gorgeous sexy hot misses waiting for me to go home to so I will see you both on opening night." Braxton's, minds racing and anxious for the day opening night arrives.

Angel looks around aimlessly with tears falling from her eyes, down her cheeks thinking about the raunchy hot steamy sex her and Zane could have here if only he would come back to her.

Braxton proud with his arms crossed over his chest tells Angel two more weeks till opening night and we did it.

I feel it in my bones that this place is going to be a roaring success and setting us on the path to riches. We should be so proud of ourselves! "You got that right Braxton!" I can see the vision now, but not only when you first said about this place I not only couldn't see it, I didn't believe it?"

"Champagne, here my friend to celebrate," "Yes please my friend!". So the two of them drank well into the night and part of the next morning!

6

Back to Work

After the commotion of the finished successful build of their sex club Knicker Box, bright and early on the Monday morning Angel fronts for her job at Fergusson's.

Waiting for her presence to arrive in her office is Storm Mason police sergeant of the local cop shop. Storm Mason is taking an added interest in Rogue Tyler and his not so well to do automotive shop.

"Hi Storm what brings you in on this early Monday morning?"

"I had to see your pretty face of course Angel!" "Okay Storm enough with the jokes what really brings you here?"

"Just thought I would touch base with you about our local con man Rogue Tyler" you were right to come to me with your suspicions Angel. His accounts compared to his spending don't add up. The business is running at a complete loss and with creditors debts mounting and a foreclosure being put in place as we speak bankruptcy is definitely on the cards. I've put my friend's private investigation company to investigate this matter, if anyone can get to the bottom of this him and his crew will. I will keep you informed after I touch base with Fishers. "Great thanks Storm I knew something was amiss!" "There's one, more thing Angel! Don't say anything or act suspiciously around him, the last thing we want is for Rogue to get suspicious that we're on to him.

Just keep things as they are and continue to work on his books!

"I will Storm and my mouth is zipped" now shouldn't you be getting back to the station to catch the real criminals?

"Bye Angel duty calls"

Wade Fergusson buzzes Angel. "Angel are you up to date with all the monthly accounts and statements?" "Yes Wade except for Rogue Tyler's" Storm Mason believes there is definitely reason for concern and has put the books in the hands of Fisher Private Investigation and Security" "Good job Angel well done!" Keep me up to date on any new information that comes to progress?" "Sure Wade, consider it done"

With the monthly reconciliations and bass and tax statements up to date Angel decides to finish for the day. She turns off her computer and light grabs her bags and shuts the door behind her and says "goodnight" to the other employees still working and heads for home.

Angel's thought process is zoned between the club and Mr Dynamite himself the one and only Zane Channing. She wonders if she will see or hear from him again. Would they ever have the sizzling explosive explicit sex they both shared over the summer? Or should she just forget about him and try to move forward? "Damn Angel, forget about Zane you're a fool to yourself" Put all your energy and focus on Night Lights and Knickerbox." Okay Mr Channing you're going to regret walking away from me and not bothering to contact me. I will show you!

Angel goes home showers and changes into her sexy leather mini skirt, thigh high boots and a tiny black leather halter top that left nothing to the imagination for the cleavage that was packed ever so tightly into the tiniest piece of leather material you could ever imagine. This will rove some wondering eyes and maybe something else too. I'm going to steam up the club tonight wolf whistles, glaring eyes and steamy sex has now taken priority focus of Angel's thoughts right now.

She arrives at Night Lights at approximately nine pm. Her entrance wows not only Braxton Miles but clientele of the club.

"Holy fucking shit Angel what are you doing?" your making me and I bet the other blokes in here steamy, hard, hot and bloody horny. Why if you wasn't my best friend I would have to take you down the back to Knicker Box and fuck you till your pussy and arse hurt.

"Geez Braxton you know that wouldn't be happening" but thanks for the compliment. "You're welcome Angel but fuck you look smashing and sexy as fuck! All I can say is Zane Channing is an idiot for not contacting you; he has no idea what he is missing out on.

"Thanks' Braxton it makes me feel a whole lot better, but I'm not sitting around waiting for Mr Hotshot handsome anymore." I'm on a mission to try Knickerbox for some unconventional, unattached pure adulterated kinky sex. After all I own half the business I may as well get some use and some of my money back out of it. Right! Right!

7

Opening Night. June 1ˢᵗ

Angel rushes out the office at precisely four thirty pm eager to get home, have something to eat, shower and put on her best sexy clothing to head out to Knicker Box's Grand Opening.

Eight pm and a cab pulls up out the front of Angel's house and beeps the horn. She has one more look in the mirror. "Well Angel you look pretty hot and sexy even if I do say so myself" Angel is dressed in a purple leather mini dress with splits at the sides, front zipper that went from top to the bottom of her dress, low cleavage at the front and no bra underneath. She wore crotch less black lace panties with black pull up fish net stockings and a pair of "fuck me,"six inch stilettos, to add the final touches to her outfit she carries a black clutch purse with a gold chain. Angel's makeup is done to perfection and she is dazzling with her glittery purple shades of eye shadows and a lollipop pink colour lipstick.

Angel throws her keys, purse and lipstick into her handbag locks the front door and jumps into the waiting cab. As the cab pulls to the front of the club and Angel pays the cabbie and steps out of the taxi, passers-by and on-lookers are ogling and whistling at Angel and her outfit and some are even shouting obscenities at her. "A job well done Angel you have accomplished the task you set out to do and achieve just the right look"

Angel arrives at Night Lights and looks straight away for Braxton. "Where's Braxton Angel asks one of their regular barmen?" "Um he was he just a minute or so ago" maybe he is out the back doing inventory? "That's ok Jason I think I know where he will be but thanks anyway" "You're welcome but Angel I must say you're looking might hot and sexy tonight!" "Why thanks Jason that's great to hear"

Anxious and nervous Angel heads out the back entrance to walk the long path that leads to Knicker Box. Shaking she opens the door to be greeted by one of their new bouncers Sam. "Hi Angel" "Hi Sam is Braxton here?" "Yep mam he sure is!" Oh my god Sam what a turnout! Who would've ever expected so many people to turn up to an event of this nature? "I guess Sam, Braxton was right" there really is a demand for this kind of market catering to the sex industry. I would never have expected to see people from such varied occupations. We have doctors, lawyers, judges, nurses, teachers, even cops all here to live out their ideal sexual fantasies.

"Well Miss Angel it just goes to show sex has no limitations or boundaries and that is what Knicker Box is all about" it's about individuals being able to express themselves individually and be allowed to act out their fantasy or play on their kinky ideas without feeling guilty or embarrassed and even more so without being labelled by the prudes of this world that still thinks sex is about the missionary position. It really does show us Miss that places such as these really are needed and greatly appreciated.

At that moment Braxton walks up to greet Angel at the entrance way in front of the door. "You are one hot, sexy fucking foxy chick there Angel" I didn't think you could look hotter than last night but fuck you've exceeded even my expectations. I can see you having no end of takers lining up to fuck you to the moon and stars and back. You will have no shortage of orgasms and climaxes here. I just wish I was one of them. There will be no stopping you tonight foxy lady.

Why I could fuck you right here right now. Just looking at you has made my cock rock hard and swollen. "Down boy or I will have to get some cold water" "Angel my cock is so hard and aching to be released just by looking at you" I need to release my throbbing ache inside of you." Well my mate that isn't going to happen with me but judging by some of our patrons I'm sure there are some willing contenders only too willing to let you rip right through the middle of them, and relieve that straining cock of yours that is bursting out of your zipper." But it certainly won't be with me. We are too good friends to cross that line and ruin what we have. Braxton we're strictly friends with a platonic friendship. "Yes I hear you and I know what you're saying but if you change your mind you know where to find me" besides what do you expect from me coming in here looking like that? "I expect you to behave and respect me" Anyway getting your mind back above your navel this is a great turnout isn't it? Yes and Braxton you right about building this place. "See I told you so" I did my homework.

One question though Braxton how do we look at these people in the face again after tonight knowing and seeing what we know? Especially considering most of them are part of our local community.

"Oh honey sometimes you're so naïve" look at tonight as though they're in acting classes and tomorrow they go back to normality doing their everyday normal jobs in their own normal world. Remember too Angel sexual gratification and deviation doesn't normally fit into "the normal category" that's why they're all here.

Tomorrow we and they will just be general people down the street or at their individual jobs. They won't think about us here and we won't think about them being here. We don't associate anyone from here outside of Knicker Box, just remember that Angel. On that note Angel I have a cock that needs to get wet and rid this raging hard on I have at the present moment so I'm off to look and find some action.

"Fine go Braxton I would hate to find you have ended up with a droopy dick before you have been laid"

For a while Angel stands near the centre of the room focusing on the orgies that are going on around her in the open arenas. There was a girl on girl. A girl and guy, multi partners including threesomes, anal fucking, cock sucking, pussy licking, tit fucking and fingering and a lot more. She was not only mesmerised and dazed she was as hot and horny as a lioness on heat. Angel could feel her juices flowing between her thighs and down her legs. Her panties although crotch less were as wet as a shag and filled with her feminine moisture. Her juices flowing readily in wait for a sexual contender to take her to a private room and fuck the arse out of her. Angel fantasises about a guy fucking her brains out until she can't breathe or orgasm any more. She wants someone to fuck her in the arse for the first time and then fuck her in the pussy, and then she can suck an engorged raging cock that's so thick she is chocking on it as he pushes deep down the back of her throat nearly cutting of her breathing. Angel envisaging suck a big thick veined cock till he's at bursting point and trembling and busting to shoot his load down her throat and past her tonsils.

At Knicker Box everyone is on a no name basis unless you're partnered or coupled. The longer Angel watches the hotter and hornier she got the moister her panties became. She guessed she could wring the moisture out of her pants they were so wet and felt like she was ready to orgasm on the spot.

Suddenly a gorgeous tall blonde haired, blue eyed with the biggest abs and physique she had ever seen wanders over to her. (He reminds her so much of Zane). "Hi" "Hi you "is all this watching got you as hot and horny as it's gotten me? "You got that fucking right!" "Do you want to come and fuck with me?" "Yes please says Angel" "Are you a private love maker behind closed doors or are you a voyeur and happy and glad for the attention?" "I'm definitely a private lover" "Well then lead the way" They both departed to a locked room. The room is dark in colour has mirrors all around the room on the ceilings and walls, with large cushions scattered over the floor and a king sized bed for the sexperts that prefer sex on a bed. There are chains hanging from the ceiling and off the walls. There are a million different types of hand cuffs and whips and wall to wall drawers filled with every kind of vibrator, anal probes, and any other type of probes, anal beads and vaginal beads you could ever possibly imagine. There a tons of tubes of gels, lubes, massage oils and thousands of packets of every type and colour condoms on the market.

Before Angel has time to think Mr Drop Dead Gorgeous has thrown Angel on the floor cushions and stripped her completely naked and has a hard erect nipple in his mouth. He is sucking hard like animals suckling milk from their mum, while his other hand is rolling her other nipple between his fingers playing with the extra sensitive areola of Angel's nipple. She is squirming and writhing with pleasure. It's so intense she feels like she is going to explode at any moment. He moves his hands down her navel and around her back licking and kissing every inch of her body as he makes his way down to the entrance of her sex. Angel begs and pleads with him to fuck her, hot and erotic and burning on the brink with desire he travels down between her legs. His tongue running through her little triangle muff. He pulls at her opening and sticks his tongue into her soaking wet pussy. He's sucking her pussy with such greedy hunger his tongue ravishing her sex. Angel's screaming stop! Please I can't hold back any longer "fuck me" please?

Mr Drop Dead Gorgeous lies on his back and forces Angel's mouth over his cock. "Suck my cock" and make me want to shoot my warm jism down the back of your throat and all down the front of you so you can leave here smelling of my masculine sex that's been left inside you and all over you. I want you to take my cock so deep in your mouth that you're gargling and losing breath. While you're sucking my big rigid cock I'm going to fuck your mouth and fuck my cock right down your throat to your tonsils. I'm going to fuck your mouth deep and hard. "What do you think about that sexy lady?"

"I love the thought of it" It's exhilarating and the most fulfilling pleasure I have ever received. "That my sweet one is because I'm the master of fucking and pleasure"

Angel starts sucking him; first she runs her tongue around the head poking her tongue down his pee hole. Sucking: wildly around the head of his cock. Then she starts running her tongue along his deep veined elongated shaft, sucking and nibbling up and down his huge rod. Gripping his balls in her hand and running her palms around his balls gathering up a hand full of ball sacks she then strokes his manhood while sucking his balls and cock at the same time. Angel rotates between his head his long thick shaft and around his balls. Wanking his cock at the same time Drop Dead Gorgeous breathing picks up as the sensation of orgasm is imminent and building up in his sperm balls. He's on the edge! Gripping tightly, thrusting and pulsating while Angel keeps sucking and fondling, she now knows he's on the verge of a volcanic eruption such a climatic orgasm just before he blows inside her he contains himself and pulls Angel away. He makes her get on her knees in front of him. She willingly obliges and strokes a condom over his super huge cock and he enters Angel's with slow small pumps each stroke gets deeper and harder. He pumps Angel's pussy with such brutal force. By now she is so totally hot and climaxed her pussy so sensitive she can't take any more cock inside her overworked pussy. "Please I've orgasmed to the maximum, your fucking amazing but I can't take any more I'm so super sensitive now. I have never endured or experienced anything like this in my entire life but can you please pull out of me now?

Mr Drop Dead Gorgeous is teetering on the brink as he pulls his erect shaft out of Angel's pussy. "I'm going to fuck you in the arse!" Have you ever been fucked annually? "No, and your too big!" How could I possibly take your length in my arse? "Just relax and trust me" I guarantee once you get over the initial pain it will be the best sexual experience you will ever receive. Trust me sexy I will enter you slowly bit by bit. You're already as wet as shag but because it is your first time experience I will make it easier by lubricating my cock so it slides right inside you. You need to push back against my cock when it is embedded in your arse hole and the more you push back on me the easier it will be for you to take my whole shaft. By pushing back on my cock you will loosen up your anal muscles so I can penetrate your tight fucking arse hole and plunge into you deeper and harder as we go. You will be so tight around my cock I will most likely shoot my load straight away down into your arse while you're climaxing with the most pleasurable fuck you have ever had before.

Mr Drop Dead Gorgeous enters her slow but deep. Angel sighs with the pain but after the initial pain she is able to loosen her muscles gripped around his solid mass that is stuck far up her anal canal and then finds she loves it. It is at this moment she begs him to fuck her in the arse hard, fast and deep. She matches him stroke for stroke. He pumps her so hard and deep and fingers her wet clitoris at the same time. The experienced Mr Drop Dead Gorgeous knows that it is not only going to send her totally over the edge it is going to crucify him until his cock shatters in her tight arse and in no time he has dumped a load of cum deep inside her and filled up the condom. Angel's clitoris is so horny and her vulva swollen with sensation and climaxed, he brings her to a climatic orgasm with his fingers and rubs some of his spilt cum into her pussy to finish her off completely. At the last penetrating stroke Angel squeals and shakes with the most eruptive orgasm she has ever been put through. Angel is lost, disorientated, satiated, tired and fulfilled and he pulls Angel into his arms to lay next to him so they can relax, take time to visualise and focus what they just shared between them and to catch their breathe. They lay next to each other covered in sweat and both smelling of sex. Neither can move their both limp with exhaustion from the hardest most sinful sex they have both ever experienced.

Mr Drop Dead Gorgeous pulls the filled condom from his now half flaccid shaft and throws it into the toilet. They both tidy themselves up and redress. Both get their breath back and share a passionate kiss and say goodnight. Angel waits for him to leave and then follows on behind. On the way out of Knicker Box and on her way home Angels wonders how she could ever possibly fall asleep tonight after the night of sexual passion she just shared with an unknown sex machine. She arrives home at five thirty am strips off climbs into bed and falls into the deepest sleep she can ever remember being in.

8

The Next Morning

ealising how tired and exhausted Angel's night of sexual passion and hard core sex made her Angel slept late into the afternoon.

The following day after a long sleep waking up feeling happy and refreshed decides the day is fading away too fast and that she needs to get up and get ready and get herself out of her place and head down town to the shops.

After her grocery shopping she walks past a new boutique. Her mind wanders to her night before, and how she would've looked with something like this on. How would Zane feel if he saw her parading around in the most provocative, sexiest lingerie she had ever seen before she asks herself? Her eyes are hugely attracted to the range of sensual items and the large range and variety and the most exquisite colour range imaginable.

The range included baby doll pyjamas, teddies, corsets, bras, fishnet and pull up stockings, suspender belts, garters and every type of knickers you could possibly ever think of from g strings and thongs, crotch less, full briefs, midi, bikini briefs, boxers and even bootleg.

This boutique carried the most luxurious colours of lingerie you could ever wish for starting with the general blacks and whites, beiges and reds. The reds ranged from rose, scarlet, crimson, maroon and burgundy. Blue colours were from the darks such as navy, sapphire and royal to the lighter pastel shades in turquoise, baby blue, sky blue, cyan and teal. Green colour ranges started from the darker forest, emerald, sea-green and then the lighter shades of lime, apple, melon and jade. In the pinks there was the dark and hot pink, coral, watermelon, lollipop, candy and in softer tones of baby pink, fairy floss and soft pink. Too many shades of purples but some were of deep and dark purple, crimson, lilacs, mauves, and lavender. With the more subtle colours in the peach, apricot, melon, lemon pale yellows to the bold prints, leopard prints, stripes and spots.

"Damn, I now I would like hot in these and after all money is in no shortage of demand for me thanks to my position at Fergusson's and her partnership in both clubs said Angel quietly to herself!" Why shouldn't I splurge a little every now and then? A couple of hours later Angel emerged from the boutique loaded to the hilt with shopping bags full of a vast range of garments in glorious stunning colours. Now all I need is a man to wear them for and Angel has a little giggle to herself.

A little after five pm, Angel crashes through her door and off loads her bags of shopping on the kitchen table and then curls up on the recliner to take a rest. Suddenly Angel gets comfortable and there is a call on her mobile. Angel answers it and it's her best friend Madison (Maddie) Carson gym junkie and total vegan. "Hi Maddie what are you up to?" "Hello my friend I've just finished a twenty kilometre run, burnt off my extra calories for the day done my full workout at the gym finished with my clients for the day and now I'm bored" I thought you might be up to some company? Maybe grab a DVD and some chips and chill out with some bottles of wine and just spend girlie time together. "Great I'm all for that, there's nothing better than chilling with your best friend on Saturday night with a DVD, some chips and a bottle of wine." "Cool I'll be over in ten!"

Angel wakes in a blur! Oh my head I feel like I've been run over by a truck! Angel gets up and soon realises they both had drank too much wine and crashed out on the lounges. It's ten am and Angel doesn't remember a single bloody thing. She takes a shower and emerges with a bathrobe on and a towel wrapped around her head.

"Why Princess you're alive and happy to make your presence known to me." "Please Angel "shush" my head is throbbing and I feel like someone has thrown a brick at my head." "It isn't any wonder Maddie we polished off three bottles of wine last night and didn't even get to see the end of the movie." "Angel I'm going to go home to Jett and have a shower and chill for the rest of the day." You don't mind do you?

"Of course not I'm going to potter around my house, do some washing put some music on and just chill out for the rest of the day also." Get all organised for work in the morning and catch an early night so I can arrive to work in the morning feeling bright and cheery.

"Okay bye Angel!" "Bye Maddie, say hi to my brother for me? "Will do!" "We'll catch up again soon."

9

Zane Channing

Monday morning the phone at Fishers Agency rings.

"Good morning, Zane Channing speaking!" "Hi Zane its Police Sergeant Storm Mason from Auburn Creek Police Station!"

"How are you going? It's great to hear from you." "It's been awhile"

"Yes too bloody long."

"Look Zane I'm sorry to be troubling you I was just wondering if you have any plans to come back down to Auburn Creek, in the very near future."

"No!" Why what's troubling you Storm?"

"I'm just going to be blunt I can't talk over the phone but I think there is some stuff going on down here and a whole lot more seems to be unfolding." I believe this is to in depth and involved for my squad back here to handle. It really needs investigating by your team of task force and the use of your private eye skills. You will also need to be doing some undercover work on this, so no one gets scared off or the town don't go into frenzy.

"Storm this sounds serious I will make the drive down there today." I should make it there by lunchtime.

"Thanks Zane I really do appreciate it, and then I can go into details with you and give you what we have stumbled on and found out." I'm also certain there is someone else who I believe may be waiting to see you again also.

"Well time will tell!" I look forward to catching up with you in a few hours. "Bye for now."

"Blake, can you come in here please?"

"Hi Zane what's up?" "I need you to get a back together we have to leave the city and travel for a case we've been asked to work on."

"Sure"; where to, and for how long? "Were, off to Auburn Creek, indefinitely." "It sounds serious." "Yes I think it is."

Blake Kristoff is Zane's best friend and business partner. They both worked on secret missions overseas together for five years. When their deployment was finished they set up Fishers Special Task Force and Private Investigation Service. They were and still are inseparable so in turn they earned the "Title of Partner's in Crime," Both watched each other's back while working special task in the battle zones of Iraq and Afghanistan.

After three long hours of driving they finally arrive in Auburn Creek.

Zane pulls up and parks in his driveway which runs right down the side to the back of his house. He definitely isn't ready to be noticed by the locals and in particular Angel Hart. He knows and feels guilty having taken off and leaving Angel hanging without any communication what so ever. Zane really isn't sure how she will react and cope when she knows what he really does for a living and even more so that he was called up for a top secret mission in Afghanistan. Zane knows Angel won't understand why he left in such a hurry, why he couldn't say goodbye and why he should've probably ended things between them before he left. He lives with that guilt every day. Due to these reasons he presumes Angel Is not ever going to forgive him let alone ever speak to him again. Again his remorse and guilt take over. "If only I had said good bye properly or did things differently."

Zane's mind continuously rolls back to the summertime when he and Angel had experienced and enjoyed the most sexually fulfilled and romantic love making either have ever endured. Now he can't believe six long months have passed since that time in his life he will never forget or even be able to get out of his system. Six long months since he last made love to and held the beautiful sexy Angel in his arms and never wanting her to leave. He knows deep down he truly loves Angel and knows he has to try to find the time to see Angel and try to put her straight and let her know he does love her more than life itself and be honest with her as to why he left and the way he did.

First things first though he has to get into the police station and see what the task is that's bought him and Blake back to Auburn Creek.

"Good afternoon, I'm Zane Channing I'm here with my partner Blake Kristoff to meet with Sergeant Storm Mason." We are both from Fisher's Special Task Force and Private Investigation Company.

"Just a minute and I will let him know you are both here said the constable, manning the front counter."

"Welcome Zane come through to my office!" "Storm this is my partner Blake Kristoff." "Hello Blake It's a pleasure to meet you!" "You're welcome sir!" "No please call me Storm."

Well guys this is Inspector Dean Reynolds head of the crime/ Fraud Task Force." Hello Mr Reynolds it's a pleasure to me you." "Back at you guys, but please call me Dean?" "Okay, but shall we get down to business?" "Absolutely, we can."

Books from Rogue Tyler's automotive shop have been brought to my attention from Miss Angel Hart, for which I believe some of you know her. Angel was put in charge to handle his contracts, books and accounts by Wade Fergusson of Fergusson's Accounting. "You all have to believe me the books not only look that bad but there is some sure signs of criminal activity being carried out. We all feel here that the shop is a front for some other fraudulent and embezzling activity that has been short changing some other businesses and also consumers of Rogue's business.

Zane questions the suspicions of the law. Why have you come to that conclusion that there are illegal dealings running through Rogue's business? We will take a look at his books that Angel's working on.

As you know Zane, Rogue lives a very lavish lifestyle, sports cars, expensive antiques, art works and million dollar houses. He fine wines and dines the ladies, drinks and gambles heavily but his accounts show negative balances. No deposits have been made into his business account. Upon doing some more checking he has huge debts with major creditors. How is he living this lifestyle, and how is auto shop still opened and operating? "Good point Storm." We will look into it right away. "Can I just ask you guys to please not say anything to Angel about me back in Auburn Creek? I need to see her and tell her in my own time my way! You have our word Zane!

Thanks Zane and Blake we know you will both get to the bottom of this. Don't forget if you need anything at all don't hesitate to ask. We all need to work together to bring this to a head. "Okay bye we will get back to you when we have something to report."

Back at Zane's house he and Blake are straight into going over Rogue Tyler's books and starting an investigation into credit and financial affairs and more so his connection to criminal activity.

"Geez Blake look at Rogue's personal debt." He has a Porsche, Ferrari, BMW, Statesman and a couple of late model 4x4's. He has a two- storey house in Auburn Creek a Penthouse on Sydney Harbour as well as an array of commercial properties including his mechanical work shop.

Here are his bank statements and he is millions of dollars in debt. He actually owes the bank more in debts than he is worth.

"Zane I think I will subpoena copies of his land titles to all his properties and his tax returns for the past decade."

"Great idea Blake I'm going to checkout all his creditors and any money or collateral he has put up to obtain these properties and fancy cars, paintings and antiques and still maintain his millionaire playboy lifestyle." Also Blake you don't need to come back tonight you can rest up and get a good start in the morning.

"Is that a call to say your busy tonight and no interruptions?"

"No not at all it's just that a good part of the day is over so we can't get much done until tomorrow now anyway." "Sure I have already checked into the local hotel anyway!" Zane, Angel really is onto something isn't she? "She sure is, she isn't just pure beauty and gorgeous she is real smart too." "Do you love her Zane?" "I guess I do but it doesn't matter now I've blown my chance I had with Angel by not being honest with her in the first place and telling her why I had to leave in such a hurry without saying goodbye and not making any contact with her since then. "If you want my opinion and by all means tell me to mind my own business if I talk out of turn but you should go find her and tell her the truth." What can go wrong with being honest?

Your right Blake it's not your business and its easier said than done! Believe me that would not be enough for Angel. "You really don't know that." "Believe me I know Angel better than anyone, I know her mind her thoughts and every inch of that super model body of hers inside and out." "Okay on that night I'll leave you with it and catch you bright and early here in the morning." "Goodnight Blake!" "Goodnight Zane!"

Zane pours a whiskey from his crystal decanter, is Blake right? Should I speak to Angel and try to put her straight about my life and the secret I've been hiding from her and regrettably regretting not telling her during our hot steamy sexy rendezvous we shared over the summer.

The more whiskey Zane drank the harder the memories to forget the more real their affair stood out, the more he realised just how much he really di love and miss Angel. Just thinking about his love tryst with Angel made his cock hard, his erection nearly breaking through the zipper of his trousers. {God Angel you're not even here and you're still able to make my cock stand to attention and make me so hot and horny.}The more I think about you the stiffer my erection gets the harder it throbs in my briefs the stronger the urge is too relieve myself. I'm literally going to come in my pants! "Fuck that was explosive!" Zane finally turns in for the night but finds he's tossing and turning. He just can't get Angel out of mind. That's it I need to go see Angel and confess my love for her and my secret and why I couldn't tell her. Most of all I need her to know that I love her and that she means more to me than any job or misguided lifestyle I have hidden from her and the deceit, why I had to leave without saying good bye but more so I can't forget what we shared and I can't move on or live without her any more.

Zane is six feet tall, broad shoulders, blond haired and blue eyed, his body his perfectly built like a nineteen fifty seven Chevrolet, his shoulders are as broad as the ocean and he has thick skin and no fear. Well maybe one is facing Angel.

10

The Meeting

Angel turns up the next morning to start her day as usual at Fergusson's. Her desk is piled high with overdue accounts, monthly and quarterly statements, Inventories and anything else you could possibly imagine. Angel absolutely hated the end of the month financial statements, meeting the budgets and the summaries that she needed ti try to keep up to date on. Angel's downfall is falling behind sometimes, especially with some of the companies more over bearing clientele. One of the only pitfalls Angel loathes about her job. Angel knows she has to try to stay focused and keep on track and try to catch up the back log of files that are now overloading her desk.

Frustrated and knowing she is in for a long day she heads to the kitchen to make herself a strong hot coffee for both Wade and herself. Angel hands Wade his coffee in his office and says good morning to him and the progresses back to her desk. "Holy Crap," how am I ever going to get through all these files and accounts in one week. Well Angel you're not going to get your work load caught up here staring at it all and moaning about it. Settling down she notices a yellow envelope sitting in front of her on her desk, and it is addressed to her yet it has no stamp or post mark so it has obviously been dropped off. Curiously she opens up the letter and dismayed and shocked she drops the letter and screams out loud. Wade and the other staff members surrounding her nearby office all come running in! Still shocked and shaken and finding it hard to speak, she manages to tell Wade to read the letter. Wade summons the other employees back to work and reads the letter.

"Your name might be Angel but you're the devil in disguise. Keep your fucking mouth shut and stay out of other people's affairs. I know where you live and I know you have been to the cops. Don't tell or show anyone this letter if you know what's good for you, you will back off!"

"Fuck me Angel what's going on?" What's this all about? Who sent you this letter? "I have no idea!" I can only think of Rogue Tyler and with me taking the information and his books to the police with the discrepancies in his books and statements.

"You really need to take this letter to Storm and ask him what he makes of all this and what he thinks you should do." "I think your right!" No I know your right I think I will take the letter to him now. "Good idea, but please Angel be careful." Wade enters back into his office and to his dismay the same envelope like Angel just received with no stamp or post mark turns up on his desk. Wade opens the letter. Oh my fucking god it's exactly the same as Angel's only mine says "You might think you're a fucking big shot accountant and thinks you know everything but you had better fucking back off or you and your family will pay the ultimate price. I know where to find your family. If you know what is good for you, you won't take this letter to the cops."

As Angel is heading down the corridor to go see Storm, Wade calls her back to his office. "Angel you better get back here!" "What's up Wade?" "Look I have a letter too." "Oh, no this isn't good, I'm starting to feel afraid now Wade." "Me too Angel, take both the

letters straight to Storm and Angel for god's sake please be careful!"
We both need to be extra vigilant. See what Storm can come up with.

It's five past nine on the Monday Morning. "Geez what a fucking
great start to the day, as if I haven't already got enough to do without
having to deal with all this shit as well." Angel arrives at the police
station. Hi I'm here to see Storm and without even asking or being
shown to his office she charges straight the desk sergeant and straight
into Storm's office.

All of a sudden she can't move her body limp and numb, heart
racing pulse rising and all of a sudden she has become completely
mute. What actually Angel came over here for suddenly isn't what is
now on her mind. Angel catches sight of those deep blue eyes, she,
they can't stop staring at each other, their look to each other is both
captivating and mesmerising, their eyes glowing at each other.

They both feel lost caught in some kind of time warp, lost in each
other's sights and their own thoughts.

"Oh dear mother of god what the fuck are you doing here?"
you're back in Auburn Creek and you didn't even have the nerve to
contact me. "You bastard I'm out of here." Storm I need to speak
with you urgently but I can't do this now. "No stop Angel this is not
the right time or place I'm here to help you." I need to speak to you
and to apologise to you but not here. Don't leave now say what you've
come to say. "Maybe we can all help." "Please Angel take a seat said
Storm." Something has you all wound up and tied up in knots to
bring you into the station by nine thirty in the morning."{Angel I
can't stop trembling! Is she trembling out of fear or because the man
she loves with all her heart, the man she gave her all self to over the
holidays is standing right beside her.} Angel knows she has to pull
herself together and tell Storm what it was she went there for in the
first instance. Storm I went into work this morning and found this
unmarked envelope addressed to me. I opened it up and this is what
the letter said. To make things worse Wade got one too. "Your name

might be Angel but you're the Devil in disguise. Keep your fucking mouth shut and stay out of other people's affairs. I know where you live and I know you've been to the cops." This is Wade's letter the same as mine but threatening him and his family.

"What do you make of this Zane?" Well for starters I'm moving Angel into my place for the time being, so Blake my team and I can protect her while we catch this bastard. Blake can keep Wade and his family safe and keep watch over them. Storm we need some more man power. We really need you to help us out here. "But I'm." "Stop right there Angel you can kick, scream and argue but I'm not taking no for an answer." You're moving in with me so I can take care of you until we catch this sick bastard. Storm I'm stepping up the investigation, when they threaten people close to me that's it!

"Zane I personally think that is the best idea!" I can't afford to have anything happening to my local people especially Angel and Wade. I also don't take these kinds of threats lightly. "I'm also going to pull Angel out of Wade's and any work or files she has to work on I will set her with everything she needs at my place." I'm also going to order Wade to take himself and his family to his house in the city suburbs until we catch this Mother Fucker. "Yes, yes Zane great idea!" I will have my men take shifts watching their houses. Zane we have to hurry up and catch this bastard!

"Blake what are your views on this?" "I feel and believe there is more than one person involved." "I agree with you." Who though and why? "Ok Storm you have to get your men in place." Let's catch this `Son of a Bitch'.

Angel is escorted out with Zane and Blake and walked back across to Fergusson's. Zane goes into Wade's office to give him the news and put their safe guards in place. In moments the staffs all briefed and now know to contact both Wade and Angel by new disposable phones ordered by Zane's firm. In no time at all their offices are both cleared out and all of Angel's supplies are filled up in Zane's Jeep and Wade's are loaded in his BMW.

Blake follows Wade home and he informs his wife and within the hour they have packed up their essentials and on the couple of hours drive to their city home. "Blake sets up security surveillance in the upper and lower levels of Wade's extravagant house in the affluent North Shore.

Meanwhile Angel continues to give Zane the silent treatment all the way home; she doesn't even give in when taken to Zane's own private house. "Angel you can't ignore me for ever." Do you want to make a bet on it?" I can have you charged with kidnapping! "I know you wouldn't do that to me, for one you know you need to be looked after and two you find me irresistible." "Don't be so full of yourself." What we had during the summer was a fling. It was nothing, more and nothing less. "Angel we need to talk!" I need to tell you why I had to leave straight away and why I hadn't contacted you. I'm willing to share my secret with you so you understand what happened and why? You can put your things in the master suite. "Oh no, I'm staying out here!" "Look there is going to be agents and officers coming here and you will have no privacy. You can stay in the master suite where everything is close by and at your leisure and I'll bunk in the study. Then if anyone comes I won't be far away from you and I can keep you at arm's length. "Then I guess you can put a collar and lead on me and take me for walks." "Don't be so sarcastic Angel you know I couldn't do that to you." "I don't need any explanations from you, we had a fling and that is the end of that." "I'm going to sit down and tell you what happened and where I was but at the moment my focus is simply on you and keeping you safe." "I'm a big girl and I don't need looking after!" "Stop acting like a spoilt brat and get used to it because I'm not going anywhere and neither are you." Now you can go and put your things away, get a feel for the house and most of all make yourself, at home and comfortable. I'm going to get Mary to fix us a nice lunch and because it's such a nice day we can eat out on the patio overlooking the pool. For now though I need to check in and make sure all safety measures are in place. My place is fully secured and monitored and that Wade's house has also had a thorough going over. Can I leave you alone for a short time without you going and getting yourself into trouble? "Oh you're such the comedian aren't you?" "No just stating the obvious!" What does my beauty fancy for lunch? "Anything for me is fine and let's get, one thing straight I'm not your beauty." "Okay Angel!" I'm not in the mood to argue, I have more important things to worry about." Bye the way Blake has set your office up in my study, all your work papers, folders, documents and computer are all set up. So there ready to use whenever you are. "Thanks Zane I appreciate what you have done, and are doing but I still think you are being over cautious and that all this is unnecessary." "Well Angel I'm sorry but I don't agree." Whoever wrote those notes aren't playing games and they are meant to be taken seriously. So until the bastard/s is caught nothing is changing.

Angel unpacks her belongings into the empty cupboards in the master bedroom and then she takes a wander into the study to check out her new temporary office. Roughly twenty minutes later Angel is greeted by a medium build woman of Filipino decent she thinks, standing in the doorway with a pale grey uniform and white full apron and white lace up shoes. Mary has dark short straight hair and dark chocolate colour eyes. She assumes this must be the maid. "Hello you must be Angel!" My name is Mary and I'm Mr Channing's (Zane's) maid. "Hello Mary it's a pleasure to meet you, how long have you been working for Zane? "I have been with him for more than five years, and I'm here to inform you that your lunch is served on the patio at Zane's request." "Thanks Mary I will be right there, I'm actually starving anyhow." She makes her way to the patio. "I hope you like avocado, chicken and lettuce salad?" "Yum my favourite." They both sit and eat and make small talk about anything and everything, about the letters, their summer romance and if only he could start the conversation about his secret.

Angel settles into her new temporary house.

11

Missing

Angel awakes and finds Zane out of the room. Great she says I'm going to do a great workout at the gym and catch up with Maddie before I put in a full day of catching up on my work over load. Angel puts on her sports gear grabs her bag and heads down the road to the gym.

Twenty minutes later Zane comes into check on Angel only to find out and realise she is nowhere in the house. "Fuck you damn fool!" What do you think you are doing? Do you want to get killed? Oh no! I have to find her before Rogue Tyler does or whoever is behind the letters. "Blake!" "Yes Zane?" "Get in here quick, I need you to get your car and search the streets for Angel." She has gone missing from the house. I'll check her office, the local shops and anywhere else I think she may have gone. You please drive around the streets!

After walking the entire local city area Zane, finds Angel working out at the gym. He walks up to her and grabs her roughly by the arms. "What the fucking hell pray tell are you doing here?" Are you fucking crazy? Do you want a death warrant marked above your head? "Oh chill out Mr Dynamite I'm just working out for fuck sake.' Everything is quite safe! "How do you know Miss Smarty pants?" Well I'm here safe aren't I? "Don't get smart with me Angel, you don't know who's watching you, or even if or who may have followed you here." "Look Zane I'm not a baby and I don't need minding!" "Like hell you don't and that is what my job is, too protect you!" Or have you forgotten that. Now get your stuff were getting out of here right now!. Zane's so furious he drags her out of the gym and practically pushes her into Blake's waiting car. "Stop it Zane your fucking hurting me." "I will continue to hurt you if you dare to pull another stunt like that again." Why did you do this, didn't you realise how scared I was to come into the bedroom to check on you only to find you gone? Angel gives Zane the silent treatment for the drive home to the so few streets back to his house. The house is in dead silence for a few hours. Finally Zane can't take anymore; he goes into the room and sits on the bed alongside Angel. He pulls Angel's face toward him so she has to make eye contact with him and look at him. Angel I'm really sorry for yelling at you and pulling at you and dragging you into the car but I was so fucking scared when I couldn't find you in the house anywhere. You have to understand the seriousness of these threats that have been sent to you and to Wade. Whoever sent those letters means business, trust me and believe in me please Angel? I beg of you I just want and need to take care of you and keep you protected. "I'm sorry Zane I really didn't think about it nor have I really taken this so seriously." It just seems so surreal to me. It's just when I woke up you wasn't here in the room, I heard you working in your office and I thought I would leave you alone to work and that it would be good to go for a complete workout and to catch up with Maddie before I got stuck into my enormous workload. I'm overburdened and overwhelmed! Zane I promise I won't do this again, not ever. I really am sorry! "That's makes me happy, that's really good. Angel I couldn't live with myself if I let anything happen to you. Both their faces were lost in the moment, both breathes, were hot, his touch was soft. In no time at all they were both naked and making hot, steamy, passionate love.

Zane kissed and licked Angel's body from head to toe, he fondled her taut erect nipples and toyed and sucked at them greedily. Zane sucked them like a baby suckling the milk form their mum. He rubbed, massage oil into her body and massaged her so slowly and sensual. All Angel could do was writhe, moan and gurgle she was euphoric in heaven and never wanting this moment to end. This is how Angel remembered the summer they both spent together. The more Zane rubbed and massaged and kissed her entire body all over, the wetter and moister her pink pussy got her. Angel was so horny and so close to orgasm she was trying to slide out from underneath him and out from his control. The more she wriggled and writhed the harder he played her. Angel begged and pleaded for Zane to 'fuck her'. "Fuck me now please I can't take any more it's so intense I'm going to explode." In that Zane buried his head between Angel's sex and rolled his tongue around the meaty flesh of her labia, sucking and licking her. He was sending her to heaven and he knew she couldn't do anything about it. Zane inserted one finger and worked her to frenzy, then he inserted a second finger and Angel could feel the magic that was building up inside her and feel the throbbing erection that was lying against her feet, and knowing she was powerless to stop him from working her to the edge; to the brink of ecstasy. No one knows how to bring Angel to a dramatic climax like Mr Dynamite himself. Never in her sexual past had she ever experienced anything so intense, gratifying so fulfilling, so climatic until Zane came along. He knows every sensitive and sexual area of her body he knows what she likes and what turns on. But mostly he knows how to make her climax so dramatically she could win an Oscar for her acting. By now Zane feels Angel's love box getting so tight and her juices flowing more rapidly than the wild rapids of Canada's wild waterways, all over his fingers. She was well on her way to coming and so tight and intense she almost broke his fingers that were buried deep inside her steaming hot, wet pussy. Angel screamed out she was exhausted, tired, sensitive; how could he bring her to such amazing climaxes just with his fingers was beyond her. (if he fucks me like this with his fingers imagine the climax with his cock entered and buried deep inside my well) she thinks to herself. The experience was not only awesome it was like nothing she had ever endured before.

Zane pulled his fingers out and knelt on his knees right over Angel's head, he filled her mouth with the biggest hardest, thickest veined cock she had not only ever seen but felt. He stuck his cock in her mouth and pushed it deep into her mouth and down her throat as far as he could get it. The more Angel opened her mouth and loosened her jaw muscles the more her mouth relaxed the more cock she was able to keep taking. His cock was so big and deep down her throat the more she gagged to try to take that bit more. Finally being completely relaxed and her jaws loosened slightly she was finally able to take his whole cock right to the end of his shaft. His balls were lying over her face and mouth. Zane pounded her mouth inch by solid inch harder and faster pulling it out and then pushing it back in stroke after stroke. Angel mouth sucking his every stroke mot missing one stroke she was sucking him as he fucked her mouth they worked in unison like it was meant to be just him and her now and for always. "Fuck baby you're making me cum!" If you keep that up I will shoot my sticky load of cum in your mouth and down your throat and you will have to swallow every last drop including what leaks out around your face and your mouth. At that very moment he spurts his white semen down Angel's throat. "Swallow it baby please don't leave any drops or excess, please baby swallow it for me?" Angel took every last drop of his sticky spunk and licked the whole of his shaft and the head of his cock clean, not wasting a drop of his tasty seed.

"Geez baby your fucking amazing!" No one except you has ever sucked my cock like you just did to me. I followed you to heaven and fuck I didn't want to come back. I came without even inserting my cock into your pink, hot ripe pussy. "Was that as good for you my beautiful one as it was for me?" "Yes, yes it was even better than the sex we had over the summer!" I have never climaxed like that in my life! "Why Mr Dynamite your cock is still hard!" "Well my beautiful one I can soon fix that." Lay on your back with your legs open and spread and hold them for me. With that Zane centred his cock at Angel's opening and rammed his rod deep inside her tight wet pussy, he had penetrated her so deep he had to pull out so he wouldn't come straight away inside her. Angel was so delirious and he had penetrated her so deep she thought he had broken through to her anus, and in no time at all Angel was tightening with such force around his hard cock. "Fuck Angel your love box is so sweet and tight I've filled it to the brim. She starts bucking back at him matching him stroke for stroke rhythm for rhythm, she gives one last buck her pussy so swollen tightens beyond his wildest orgasms, he can now feel his balls starting to tremble and he knows he is on the brink, right on the edge and about to let loose inside of her. "Hold on babe I'm coming inside you, I'm filling you with my seed, and with that he shot his load inside of her tight fully climaxed pussy. They both came together and Zane pulled out of her.

Both of them over worked and extremely and totally exhausted they roll over, Angel in Zane's arms they both drift off to sleep together.

12

The Morning After

Angel wakes up to the smell of hot roasted coffee, pancakes with maple syrup and bacon and eggs sunny side up. "Good Morning my sexy lady!" "What, what time is it?" "It's a little after nine; "At night!" "No! Gorgeous it's the next morning!" "Holy shit 'how did I sleep all that time?" "I don' know but you did, I think I wore you out yesterday, and besides you haven't had much sleep in the past few days." "What's this Mr Dynamite?" "Breakfast fit for a princess." "But aren't we eating out on the patio?" "No I thought I would treat you, seems you treated me to the best time of my whole life yesterday." "Angel blushes a crimson shade of red!" "Did you enjoy it my beautiful one?" "Enjoy is an understatement!" I can't tell you how many times I climaxed, it was the most exhilarating and convulsive explosion I have ever experienced and enjoyed. Maybe that is why I slept through to the next day. "Then just imagine my beautiful one that was just a sample of what you're going to be getting from me for the rest of our life together." "What time did you wake Mr Dynamite?" "I guess a little after eight even though I was awake for some time earlier before that just lying and admiring how beautiful and peaceful you look asleep in my arms." "Are you going to eat with me?" "I most certainly am!"

Zane, can we talk? There's something I need to ask you? Something I really need to know if I'm to go down this forever path with you. "Is it why I left without saying goodbye or not contacting you?" "Yes!" "Angel it's complicated and your right I do owe you an explanation, it's just the timing isn't right just at this moment." "But, but." "No but's Angel but I promise to reveal all to you in due time." First things first we need to catch the son of a bitch whose leaving those threatening letters around. That I assure you Angel I won't tolerate! "Okay I guess I can wait but please, Zane did I do anything to you? Did I not make you sexually fulfilled? Was I just another fling to you? 'Stop it! Stop it Angel, Zane grabs her arms and puts her arms around his neck, looks straight into her eyes and says no, none of the above." You were not the reason at all I left town and no matter what; I don't ever want you to think it had anything to do with you. You did more than sexually gratify me, in fact you blew my mind, no way could you ever be just a fling to me, I had not spent one hour of any day thinking about you what we had what we can still have and who we are as a couple. All I could think about was loving, you and being in love with you. For fuck sake, just thinking about you got me so fucking horny I couldn't even think straight. I got a boner thinking about you every day and you still have this effect on me now. I was so angry and depressed thinking about what I had to walk away from and leave behind, it tortured me; like a knife through my heart. Everyday having to live with the guilt of not saying goodbye, how much you meant to me but mostly how much I loved you. Angel I promise when this is all over and know you, your brother, Wade and his family are safe I swear I will lay all the cards out on the table and tell you everything. Angel you must know and understand though that I love you more than I could ever love anyone else and I have never felt like this before, nor could I ever love another. You have my heart, soul, and my anything, that

I have and all that I'm. The one thing that would kill me, if I knew you didn't feel the same about me and that you couldn't see a future with us. "Zane I fell in love with you the first I laid eyes on you!" my guts and heart though were cut out when I was just shut out of your life no contact at all, not even a phone call or a message." You mean everything to me also, your all I could think about all I wanted, I guess in all honesty I think after not hearing from you in so long I was looking for closure but couldn't stand also thinking what we had was over before it really got started.

"Angel my beautiful one, your my lover my life and I hope in the not too distant future you will be not only my wife but the mother of my, no sorry our children." "Oh! Zane there hasn't been a day or minute go by that I haven't thought about you, us and what we shared. It's something of a spiritual love and it sits deep in our hearts." I thought after hearing nothing from you for months you must've had your way with me and then moved onto your next conquest and I bet there are no shortages of them! "I will tell you now my beautiful one, I will always love you and only you and I promise to always be true to you and although I can't promise I won't go away any more, I will be here right alongside you every other moment excluding our work. Now can we get off this subject and eat our breakfast before it goes cold? "Yes, Mr Dynamite and I do truly love you with everything I have to give plus some more." "I don't expect nor do I want any more than just you as you are?" "Just one more question please?" "Okay one only and that's it!" "Fine can I take a drive away today? I've been couped up here and I just need some fresh air and get away for a bit. "Definitely no definitely not, but I will drive you Angel any place you want to go." "Do you really mean it?" "Yes I will drive you anywhere your heart may desire, so if you want to go you better hurry up and eat and then hop in the shower and get yourself ready." Don't take too long or we will be late getting away. Bye the way you may want to pack a few clothes because I think we're going to stay away for a few days. With that Angel jumped up put her arms around Zane and kissed him passionately. Okay Miss you better get in the shower because look what you have done to me. If you keep this up I just may need to take you right here right now. Then we will never get away. With that Angel lets her release go from around Zane's neck and as she turns away he gives her a slap on her backside. Angel we're leaving in thirty minutes! "Yes sir, aye captain, and Angel give's Zane the sarcastic captain's salute."

"Blake hi It's me Zane!" "Hi Zane, what's up?" "Well Miss beautiful is getting bored just hanging around here so I'm going to take her away for a few days just in case she decides to do something silly." Can you please hold down the forte here while I'm away? "Sure can!" "Also please make sure the guys take extreme caution with Wade and his family." Keep me up to date with any leads or progress that comes to hand and of course any new developments!" "I will Zane it will be all hands on deck here." Thanks Blake and remember I'm only a phone call away, you can ring me at any time of the day or night." "How long do you think you will be gone?" "That depends on the boss lady or if there are any changes in the case here, but I'm guessing most probably a few days to week, but I will check in every day." "Consider it done Zane, have a good time away with that gorgeous lady of yours and don't worry about anything back here, me and the guys have got it all covered!".

Twenty minutes later their bags were packed and in the car and them both were on their way.

"Zane you haven't told me where you're taking me!" "No and I'm not going to now either, it's a surprise. "Can you at least give me just a little hint?" "No my beautiful one you will just have to be more patient and wait!"

Angel cuddled into Zane as they were driving along and as they got out on the main highway along a long stretch of road, Angel pulled Zane's fly down and pulled his cock out, put her head down played with the head of his cock and stroked and rubbed it up and down. She had the whole of his cock in the palm of her hand as she stroked it and tickled the head of his now fully erect beast and before Zane could even take a breath she went down on him sucking his man rod taking him whole, swirling her tongue around it, driving it up and down his erect shaft, licking his knob licking and nibbling at his hole on the head of his cock, driving him totally in sane. Angel was insatiable, so desirable all Zane could do was try to concentrate on driving while knowing she was bringing him to the brink, she had him on the edge of shooting his jism and filling up her gorgeous mouth with his seed of love. Angel took to his man rod like flies to rotten meat; she took him whole, right to the end of his shaft till his balls hung around her mouth. Although Zane's cock was so enormous she was not going to settle on anything less than his whole girth till his balls we're bouncing around and hitting her cheeks till she gagged and choked on his rod of love. She licked and sucked his manhood from top to bottom and down each side, passing all the huge veins that defined his huge erection. Angel knew Zane was near the end of his tether and trying so hard to keep his mind on the road but she didn't care. All she could think about was giving some of her love making skills back to Zane and have him freeze with empowerment, overjoyed with sexual lust, taking him somewhere he hadn't been before, to the point of no return. Seeing Zane cringe and moan was making her even more wet and hornier than she could ever imagined and knowing Zane knew how hot and wet and horny she was made him even hornier than he thought could be possible. "Baby if you keep that up I swear I'm going to come down your throat and leave a mess all over the front of my car!" "Don't worry honey I bought towelletes to clean up so you and no one else would ever know I blew you in the car." "With what you're putting me through I hope you know revenge is going to be sweet!" "Is that a threat or a promise?" "That miss beautiful one is definitely a promise!" "With the last lashing from her tongue over his penis head and playing with the tip she could feel Zane's cock increasing by the second and stretching himself out in the car with no escape and nowhere to go quivering and shaking like he had an itch in his pants he couldn't reach to scratch and with that Zane yells "oh fuck baby that's it I can't take anymore, I'm going to come!" he pulsates and shakes, his erect cock throbbing in her mouth and in no time at all he shoots his carnal seed straight down the back of her throat. Angel's mouth is full of his white sticky seed that Zane so willing ejaculated into her mouth as she swirls it around inside her mouth and swallows the lot.

The excess that spilled around her mouth she wiped with the towellettes she packed, she carefully tucked his stick semi-erect cock back in his trousers and zipped him backup. Angel tidied herself up, wiped the seats and sat back in her seat. "Wow babe that was the best damn blow job I've ever had." I'm just letting you know what you're in for on our time away. I will be fucking your pussy, your anus and your mouth and you will be pleading me for mercy! "Gee I'm getting all hot and wet just thinking about it, I can't wait."

"Are you hungry Angel, because if you are we can stop at a roadhouse and have lunch?" "No I'm fine!" I can wait till we get to our destination; wherever that maybe. With that Angel gives a bit of a yawn. "Are you tired my beautiful one?" "Yes I'm a bit." "Well lay your seat back and have a snooze, we still have a few hours to go to reach our destination." With that Angel had adjusted seat back and in no time at all had drifted off into a deep sleep. Finally after another couple of hours driving Zane spots the exit turn off. Highway One! Next exit St. Leonards. As Zane drives past the local shops, down past the main street at the top of the hill, Angel awakes. "You've awoken Sleeping Beauty!" "Where are we?" watch Angel as we come over the hill and start heading down you will see the most glorious coastline I bet you have ever seen. Oh my god Zane it's beautiful! The water is so crystal clear and the sea has a perfect colour selection of blues and greens to magnificent shades of turquoise and aqua. I have never seen anything so beautiful and clean and the beach sand is so pure white it looks virginal. "How did you know about this place? It's my place I brought it over five years ago as my home away from home. Unfortunately, I don't get back here nowhere near as much as I should. "It's so bloody beautiful, it's like a fairy-tale." Zane turns into a long driveway where the house is nearly disguised behind the most awesome fully foliaged trees and huge wrought iron gates similar to what you would expect to find around a compound. At the start of the driveway stands a big sign, which says Channing's Retreat on the right hand side to the entrance gates. The Heritage looking cottage, (no it's too big to be a cottage) 'Says Angel" with a full bull nosed veranda the whole way around the house. The cottage itself is set back deep into the property off the main road and right at the bottom of the long track that takes you right to the back of the house. Angel is in complete awe! Never in her entire life has she ever encountered such prestige luxury, something so beautiful and with so much clarity and charm. Not only does it overlook the sea it has a magnificent kidney shaped, crystal clear pool with an adjoining spa. The yard is exquisite with every type of tree and shrub you could possibly imagine, and the flower beds are so immaculately manicured and flowers in full bloom with everything in the garden from irises, pansies, carnations, roses, tulips and snap dragons and way to many more to mention. On the other side of the pool fence is this gorgeous quaint red oak building with a red tin roof. "What's that for Angel asks with a bud of excitement in her and just a touch of naivety?" "That my dear is a sauna, gymnasium and full bathroom and changing facilities!" "And to think you called this a cottage, well I'll be damned." "Well yes! What else would it be?" "A luxurious resort." Please Zane tell me we can stay here forever! Believe me Angel if it was possible we would. "But I guarantee when you agree to marry me and have my children we will definitely spend most of our life time here and commute back to Auburn Creek for visits." "Mr Dynamite you've got yourself a deal!"

Three days into their stay Blake calls Zane! "Hi Zane it's me Blake!" "What's up dude?" "Well there has been some more threatening letters posted around town." "Too whom?" and what do the letters say?" "Again no post mark they were dropped into Storm's office at the cop shop. There's one, each for Wade, Angel, and one for you me and the lads." "What do the letters say?" "They say the same as the first ones, only this time they threaten Fisher Security, telling to back off and stay out of other people's business and to "Fuck Off", or Angel, her brother Jett, Wade and his family are all dead." "Fucking Christ, now what do we do?" I should come straight back but then that would put Angel in jeopardy and I'm certainly not going to do that; and I can't leave her here by herself either. "No I agree Zane I think it would be in yours and Angel's best interest for both of you to stay put and keep yourself and Angel safe!" I have Wade and his family covered. "Well that's something I don't have to worry about." Okay can you fax me the letters but firstly make Storm send them over to forensics for fingerprinting and see what might come back from them? I also need all of Rogue Tyler's books couriered over to me. I'm going to look over them again from top to bottom and see if there are any clues to work with or if we could be missing something of great importance. In the meantime hang low, keep an eye on Wade his family and the other's back home and make sure the guys are well placed on surveillance to observe all his coming's and going's, and in particular keep an eye on Angel and Wade's houses. "Consider it done!" "Is there anything else before I go?" "Also you need to watch your back and keep safe!" One more thing please report into me every day and remember if I'm busy, then leave a message. "I have received that loud and clear!" until tomorrow then Zane, see you later.

Zane where are you? "I'm here in the kitchen making us some lunch." What is wrong my beautiful one? "You have been gone so long I wasn't sure what you were doing." What are we having? Can I come in and help you get lunch sorted? "Nope, I have it all covered." Do you want to eat on the patio? "That would be great; the weather is just so perfect today." "How was your swim?" "Absolutely invigorating, the pool is crystal clear and glorious." "I'm so glad my beautiful one, I love to watch you swim but more importantly I love watching you in that extreme mini bikini, that leaves nothing to the imagination. It really turns me on. "Who couldn't possibly be happy here Zane? It's like being on a permanent vacation." Speaking off which is this coming to an end in the next day or so? This week has just gone so fast. "Sit and eat and we will talk." "Talk about what?" What's wrong? "I spoke to Blake before and it seems some more letters have turned up." So I thought we would make our stay here indefinite. Is that is okay with you? "Of course, I couldn't think of any place better than here or anyone I would rather be held up with than you, Mr Dynamite!" I would have thought though you would rather do your investigating from Auburn Creek instead of here. "No because that would put you in danger and jeopardise our mission." I will work from here as will you and Blake and the guys will oversee and watch out in Auburn Creek. "Yummy lunch smells exquisite!" What is it? "Thai Green Curry and rice and then I have made you a nice Tiramisu cake for dessert." "Do I get a second dessert asks Angel as she rubs her feet up and down Zane's legs at the table and gives him a cheeky grin and a wink." "You my beautiful one is going to get a second dessert but it's not going to be Tiramisu, it's much nicer." "Gee I can't wait!

13

Channing's Retreat

After lunch they tidied up took all the dishes inside and stacked them in the dishwasher. Zane decided to take Angel for a complete tour of the grounds. Angel, are you up for a walk around the grounds and then a stroll along the beach? "Absolutely", how close is the beach? "About half a kilometre, we get to it from the end of my property boundary line. "Just give me ten minutes to slip my summer dress and sandals on." "That I will my beautiful one because I don't want any other guys looking at that super-hot body." Otherwise I may end up getting that jealous, that I could end up killing them. "You don't need to worry my body is all yours and I'm definitely not interested in anyone else." "I'm glad but all the same I still want that gorgeous body covered up." "Aye Captain and again smugly gives Zane the captain's salute." "Forgive me my beautiful one but what is this salute the captain thing in aid of?" "Does it piss you of my sensitive little man?" "It kind of does actually!" "Build a bridge and get over it and have a cry my sooky waa waa!" With that Zane grabbed Angel by the arms, embraced her tightly and kissed her passionately, his kisses were long and sensual and on the occasion he put his tongue down her throat, waiting for Angel to reciprocate the kiss right back, and she did, every move he made she returned kissing his neck, all the way down his back and belly and licking around his navel leaving Zane with a tingling sensation running through his body. It struck him like a lightning bolt only with more pleasure and intensity, and he knew by now he had grown rock hard his weapon waiting to be parked tight into the waiting shed. Angel was relentless kissing him all over, licking and sucking at his face and lips, licking through the masculine hairs on his chest, she could feel his bulk rubbing up against her leg and she knew how much she was sending him over the edge as he was with her. The moisture between her legs was oozing, her panties wet, and love nest moist, steamy and horny and ready to take Zane's manhood deep inside of her. She wanted him to torture her with his weapon as only he knows how to satisfy her. They are both voracious and hungry for each other for knowing what's about to become. This is what brings them in unison when Mr Dynamite parks in the very tight shed. Next Zane pulled Angel onto the sunbed, stripped her naked while she pulled his clothes off with such fierce, and impatience, she wanted him all of him right now, as far and as deep as he could park inside her. They were at it like two lion's on heat fighting for the prize female. Their bodies were entwined, their arms and legs twisted around each other, both fearful not to let go of the other, their love making is carnal, wild, fierce the love scent from their bodies were strong and odours filled the room. "I can not only tell your horny I can smell your perky little love box, baby it's sets me off it makes me go crazy for you. I love you, your body your scent and I love filling you with my muscle drink to quench your thirst." "I Love the way you fill me up, satisfy me, send me over the edge where there's no going back. I love the smell of your body odour mixed with your body sweat saturating into my flesh, it brings out the animalistic qualities in us, the rage of adrenalin that shoots through our bodies like a Tsunami following an earthquake, but most of all Mr Dynamite I just love you. "Baby my cock is so hard it's throbbing and your pussy is so wet the love juice is filling up all over my cock like a waterfall, your pussy is so tight I don't think I can hold back any longer, the effect you have on me is always too strong for me to try to stop or slow down my climatic urge." "I know baby I'm coming I'm fulfilled, satisfied, delirious, ever so sensitive babe, I'm coming I'm over the edge now please babe come inside me now fill me with your love juice, oh baby please, I can't take anymore." "I'm sorry honey you will have to beg harder than that!" "Oh Zane please insert your cock into my pussy and fuck me like there's no tomorrow, I want you to make me come as only you know how to bring me to the most climatic orgasms ever experienced." I promise you if you stick your big cock inside my tight wet pussy, I will not only come all over your cock and make you climax with me, your sperm will be leaking out of my very well fucked pussy and dripping down the inside of my legs. "There my darling those were the magic words, and in no matter of time at all Zane was fucking her furiously deeper and harder, the vigour and force was splitting Angel in two. Angel matched him stroke for stroke. He pushed it in harder and harder, relentless; she was numb yet could still feel what was happening inside of her, fuelled by passion. By now they could both feel the orgasm building Angel was delirious, dazed, fulfilled, yet still waiting and wanting more. "That's it my beautiful one I'm coming, coming so deep my cock is pulsating like vegetables in a blender, oh, oh I came inside you baby." "Sex is just so intense between us honestly my beautiful one it gets better every time, but then who wouldn't enjoy fucking a beautiful lady like yourself with the most sensitive and tightest pussy in the world." I feel like the luckiest man in the world! "And I sir am the luckiest girl in the world!"

Angel needed Zane, needed what he gave her love, satisfaction and most of all affection. Zane needed Angel for pretty much the same reasons but selfishly because he wanted her, and could control her and attend to her every whim but getting what he needed the most out of her, her love and her pleasure the way she killed him slowly, but passionately, gratifying him insatiably. "Oh my god, Zane I don't know you always manage to keep doing that to me?" I actually see stars as you brink me to the brink of climaxing. "Well my beautiful one it's easy to fulfil your needs when you're as hot as fuck as you are, and your pussy puts out that odour of yours and gets that tight it crushes my dick and nearly cuts off my blood supply and ignites my sperm so that I fill you up with my calling." You make it easy for me to satisfy your needs as you do mine!" Now quick go and tidy up and let's go take that walk.

Zane's property sits on one thousand acres and it is absolutely glorious. They both walk down towards the southern end of his property which looks onto the beach shore line. There is every tree imaginable planted along the fence line and a phenomenal raised garden bed in the centre of the property. In it sits a magnificent solid marble statue surrounded by some of the prettiest flowering plants you could ever imagine. Running in a circle around the garden bed is the prettiest sprays of carpet roses in tones of lavenders, apricots and yellows.

"My god Zane this is not a cottage it's a flipping palace, I've never seen anything like this in my life except in the movies." "Well my beautiful one this is all yours!" "What do you mean this is all mine?" "I want you to marry me?" Will you marry me please Angel? "I love you Zane and marrying you is what I've always dreamt about but I can't say yes yet!" "Well why not?" "Because Zane we still haven't had that talk yet, and I still wake up every day thinking that you're going to be gone again, no messages, no phone calls nothing." I'm still so insecure because of it and I know I just couldn't go through that again with you gone for weeks or months at a time and never knowing if you're ever coming back. I'm sorry Zane I can't put up with that again and I won't put myself through it ever again.

"I know my beautiful one I owe you an explanation Angel but you have to believe me I never stopped loving you or thinking about you every day." I just had something to do and I couldn't tell you or even let you know where I was. Baby Angel I promise to talk to you and tell you my secret and I can promise you from the bottom of my heart I won't ever leave you again. If the need does arise I promise I will be straight up front and honest with you. All I need is your promise that you would still be here when I do get back and that you will always be here when I return. I couldn't imagine my life without you!

"I can't make that promise until I know what and where you went and why you cut me off?" "Okay I will make a deal with you my beautiful one, let's put this aside for now and finish enjoying our walk and tomorrow we will talk!" Deal! "Deal"

They both walked arm in arm heading towards the gates at the back of the property that heads out to the beautiful blue beach and the whitest crystal like sand you could ever wish to see. On the left hand side of the property next to the gates was a tennis court that could also have volley ball played on as well. To the right was a mini golf course. "Geez Zane you play golf?" "I used to play but don't get much time these days!" I used to play a lot more years ago.

Together they cross over the road and down the long walkway; and right there in front of Angel is the most glorious ocean and beach she has ever laid eyes on. "So my beautiful one what do you think?" "I think you have underestimated this cottage." It is more a tropical resort with ocean views and palatial surroundings. That's what I think! Angel just in complete awe of her surroundings lay on the sand in Zane's arms kissing and cuddling. "My beautiful one we had better make our way back now it's getting late and I want to make you a beautiful candlelight dinner." "Zane I have a heavy work load I need to catch up on also." "Not tonight Angel, you can get a fresh start in the morning." They returned to the house around five thirty pm and Angel showered and fixed herself up while Zane prepared dinner for them both.

At six pm, Angel stepped into the kitchen looking as radiant and sexy as ever. "My beautiful one how do you manage to do this to me?" "Do what to you?" Walk out looking like that, I will have to fuck you before tea!" "No Zane you need to keep calm and chill out and wait till tonight!" "How can you say that to me when you always dress so provocatively and make me so hot and horny?" "Provocatively, I have a pair of shorts and a t-shirt on." "Yes but it's the way you wear it and what's underneath it that does it to me." "Oh Zane, you're incorrigible." "You Angel my beautiful one, is just to fucking hot and sexy for words." Now sit down at the dining table and I will serve our dinner.

Their first course was a prawn cocktail with fresh prawns straight from the sea, and a crab meat and garden salad. "Mmm, yummy, Zane where on earth did you learn to cook so well?" "Well you see my beautiful one if I gave away my secrets, I would most probably have to kill you." "Well don't do that or I won't live to taste the other courses on the menu." "Smart arse says Zane reflectively!"

The second course was a rack of lamb with a marinade of seeded mustard and mint sauce and a hint of rosemary, orange and honey glazed carrots, Idaho potatoes, which are potatoes baked in the jackets with a topping mixture of sour cream, grated melted cheese and chives and a sprig of parsley and all were served with a medley of fresh steamed vegetables. This is better than restaurant quality Mr Dynamite, I'm shocked but excited and loving every bit of it. "Well then that means I must be doing my job properly then hey?"

When Angel takes the metal warming lid of her main course she sees something sparkling between the lamb racks and the Idaho potato. She picks it up and right before her eyes is a 2 carat white and pink diamond engagement ring with the rarest pink diamonds you would ever see. "Wow, wholly fuck, this must've cost you a fortune, it is simply stunning the prettiest thing I have ever seen." The stones are dazzling and shining in the light, but Zane you need to take it back I already explained to you why I can't marry you. Believe me I would love to keep it and wear it but that would be hypocritical of me and that is reason enough I can't keep it. "Angel I know what we discussed but I'm a very convincing person and I'm not going to take no for an answer." Either way you will become my wife and you my beautiful one will bear my children, so I want you to wear this ring and tomorrow we will talk and by then you will be ready to accept my proposal. "So please Angel put the ring back on?" "Okay Zane but if I don't get the answers to the questions that have been haunting me for months then I take the ring back off and you take the ring back to the jewellers." "Deal" "Deal"

Eating her meal Angel can't help but admire the ring and keeps holding it up to light to watch the diamonds sparkle and glisten. "I must say Mr Channing you really do have exquisite taste but I really don't know how you can afford your luxuries on your security wage." "Tomorrow Angel everything will become more clearer and you will soon understand." The only question I ask of you my beautiful one is what do you think of the ring? "Words can't explain how I feel, I have never seen anything so exquisite and luxurious and expensive, and it fits like it was made just for me. I do so hope I like or can accept what you are going to tell me tomorrow because I'm going to find it very difficult to take this ring off and give it back.

With their main course all cleared away Zane brings out the third and last course for the evening, dessert. It is a lemon meringue pie served with hot custard and cream. "Dinner was magnificent my man, I can't believe how domesticated you really are?" does this keep up if we marry or are you just out to impress me? "No Angel you will never have to cook a meal or wash a dish again." "I think I could enjoy this lifestyle, and how perfect is my life at this very moment?" "This is just the start of what's in store for you my beautiful one."

With dinner over and dishes done they both retreat to the sitting room to watch television with Zane wrapped around Angel in a tight embrace they both drift off into a deep sleep.

14

The Secret

The next day they both awoke embraced in each other's arms; "well Mr Dynamite today is the day!" it will decide on whether we have a future together. "I'm happy my beautiful one to tell you everything, to come clean about my past and it is also your chance to come clean and confess anything I should know about you.

Mr Dynamite this was never about me it was always about the way you left for no reason, your lifestyle, your wealth and anything you might have closed away.

True Angel but in order for us to build a future together we both need to come clean about our pasts and have no secrets that can come back to haunt us later. "Not that I'm saying you have any secrets from me; do you Angel? If though you do, now is the time for us to air out our dirty laundry so to speak, lay our cards on the table and put everything out there for us to deal and work with together.

Now Angel where do I start? "Try the beginning Zane it's always easier to start at the beginning."

Well the reason I had to leave you was because of my job, and not what I actually told you. "You see Angel I'm a private eye but mostly I'm a secret agent in the Special Forces service and a lot of my work is top secret and undercover." "Like a type of James Bond." 'Yes sort off; I'm sent overseas to interrogate and infiltrate the enemies." I have to force them to tell us their armies, or countries plans and secrets, of any terrorist plots that could be in the planning, whether they (the different countries) could be planning to send troops into ambush a particular place or whether they could be getting a strike force ready to take control." Sometimes it can be just as simple as leading the way to bring home prisoners of war who had be captured and need to be set free or to return and or identify a dead body that could off been killed during active duty or taken by the enemy in a raid or ambush. Another part of my job is to sometimes search for missing service men and women and also to be involved in peace talk where countries are heating up with a threat of combat strike or even war. Sometimes it is also my job to report and identify victims and casualties of war and report to the Captain of the Special Intelligence Forces that is heading up that particular investigation.

My job also has me working a lot of times undercover like what I'm doing now to catch whoever it is that is sending out the death threats or working so the enemy is unaware that they are under surveillance and being ambushed and in the most dramatic of cases and statistically a very minimum feat is to kill them. "Why would you kill innocent people? I just can't comprehend this in you, I would never in my wildest dreams have suspected this from you, let alone know that this is what you're paid so highly to do. I understand the high pay because of the risks you take but I can't get my head around you being the most gentle, romantic loving guy here with me, who is hell bent on keeping me protected at any cost but to know you go overseas to kill people is just fucking insane. I actually feel scared around for the first time ever being around you. "What would you do if you come face to face with whoever is threatening me and Wade?" Just shoot to kill; oh my god. To think my worst fear was that you went overseas to pick up with another family you have hidden away. Trying to keep up with a life away from here and then me here!

Angel my beautiful one you're not understanding what I'm telling you! Sometimes we need Special Forces to kill the enemy first. They are terrorists, rebels, militia or missionaries set to fight for their country at any cost, their whole ideals are brainwashed into being powerful and in control, wanting to take other countries from the empowering corporate body so they can take over and rule other countries and build their empires. They build up their array of worshippers willing to fight and even die for their own countries leader for their own country. This Angel comes at a big cost to many who suffer such as continuing wars breaking out, innocent victims being killed or at best held hostage. There are people being tortured to gain information about any leaks or leads to the countries which are in the firing line of take overs and rebellion by foreign dictators, rebels and militia.

I have spent the past ten years commuting between Iraq, Afghanistan, America and Australia and I have changed a lot of processors that had been put in place, but I have also lost some battles both personally and professionally. Never once though have I given up the fight for not only the allying countries but for their people's civil liberties and freedom in other countries, the simple things you and I here take for granted.

At the fall of Iraq I saw so many deaths by Iraqi soldiers and the Allies, these deaths were not all soldiers in war most were innocent civilians definitely in the wrong place at the wrong time and all because one leader Saddam Hussein wanted more power and control and take over non Iraqi countries and possess all the oil supplies in the Middle East and he wanted to turn all his beliefs into the whole countries people's beliefs.

Society gives our fellow man freedom, freedom to vote, speak and to believe in our own way of life, it allows us to be different and to be able to make our own decisions and choices, choices that these Non Democratic countries don't have. They are dictated and have to live by that law or belief. Countries like Iraq, Iran, Saudi Arabia, Lebanon and Afghanistan, their people aren't allowed to live with freedom, be able to speak their minds or voice their opinions or have choices. Their civil liberties are taken away by each countries individual leader dictating their power and control over each of the countries. If we don't like something or disagree with how we think things should be, we have choices, such as call an election to remove the Governing Power from their position, or we can protest. These people in these countries die for the same kinds of choices we make on a daily scale. You my beautiful are a fine specimen and a good example of what I'm trying to get through to you, you are a powerful working woman and business woman, who has gotten where you are today partly because of your freedom of choice has allowed you the right to do what you want, go where you want, wear what you want, say what you think and work because your allowed.

These Arabic countries that are ruled and powered by men, and women's rights and choices mean nothing. The world has changed and evolved in the way they view people's choices globally. These non- democratic countries can now see how much women have been introduced into culture, the work force and power and want to see these countries relent and offer women's rights and freedom (speaking for mainly the women in these countries). The people of these countries have seen how freedom and choices has changed the way the world operates today for example there are women flying planes, going into space, running countries in politics. Three high- powered women that first come to my mind are Margaret thatcher, Hilary Clinton and Australia's own Julia Gillard. This would be a death sentence if you put any of these women in any of those countries.

During my tour of Iraq and Afghanistan I came across some horrific events including imprisoned women who have been in jail for some as long as twenty years, all because they did something that was taboo or forbidden in their country. One such story that sticks in my head even to this day is a woman who went to prison because she ran out of her house to chase their three year old son who had gotten out of the house and ran across the road without a Burqa on her head. She is serving twenty years. This woman who for this sake we will name Fatima was one of the worshippers that believed in the over turning off the Saddam Hussein Government in the hope that Iraq could become more modernised and that women be given equal rights and choices. To have the choice to wear clothing from the western world and not have to leave the house wearing a Burqa and to be able to get a job in the work force. The political regimes want the power to turn their beliefs into our westernized civil beliefs and rights. The wars that are ongoing through these countries now shows that the majority of their population don't want to live that life any more when they can have the choice to live in a more modern civilised culture, a more non-lifestyle disciplined and unregimented and totally free lifestyle where they can follow a career path, watch television, listen to the radio go to theatre and concerts all the things that we take for granted that are still forbidden in most of these countries today. "You must've seen lots of tragedy in your life and especially overseas?" How has it affected you personally? You know Zane I'm here to listen; I will always be here to listen to you no matter what it is or what time it is! Thanks Angel and believe me in time I will open up and tell you things, and there are something's I'll never be able to tell you be the wounds cut to deep.

"Why couldn't you have just told me this all before?" Mainly Angel a lot of my work is top secret and some of the countries, territories and roles I have had to play have also been top secret, and that is probably the biggest reason I hadn't told you the truth, and there have also been times when I've had to go on a mission and the risks had been so high and intense the reality was that there was a big chance I was never coming home.

"I'm sorry Zane you're talking about marrying me and me bearing your children but I can sit here and honestly tell you that I can't and won't live this lifestyle. Every time you walked out the door to go on a mission with the thought of possibility that you're never coming home to me or the children. I can't live like that! I won't! What are your plans for the future? Are you still working as a Special Agent.? Do you need to go back overseas? "Geez Angel my beautiful one too many questions at once, slow down and one question at a time!" Firstly I have resigned from my position as a Special Agent and I'm totally focused on my business partnership with Blake running our PI and security business. As for your second question I'm hoping my future involves you in my life for ever. "I love you Angel; I've loved you since our first encounter and since meeting you I had come to realise you complete me in every way possible, or nearly in every way possible! Since I've been with you I made the conscious decision about how challenging and dangerous my love was and had become. I would get called away at no notice to go god knows where and each time I could never really guarantee when or if I would come back home. After meeting you all my responsibilities and priorities changed, I want to be able to have a life where my beautiful wife and kids are home to greet me every night when I get home. I want to be able to read to my kids every night and tuck them in their beds and kiss and cuddle them every night. My before life would never allow me to do this. I want to sit on the sofa cuddled up with my wife with the lights dimmed and the candles burning with my wife wrapped around me and embracing me while we kiss and cuddle before we go off to make the most beautiful love that only you and I can do, and I want his every night not just on occasions. Angel I want and need the whole package, the wife, the kids the house and everything that goes into making us a whole as a union, joined to each other and to our children we bring into this world together our creations. For your last question I won't say I will never go overseas again but it would be for different reasons and I would be safe. I also know I couldn't go for very long and leave you behind; I can't stand not seeing you after five minutes imagine what it would be like if I'm away longer. Leaving you behind would be like putting a spear right through my heart and I would die slowly. Just one thing I must iterate if I knew I had to go overseas for a lengthy amount of time then you and the kids would undoubtedly accompany me.

"My beautiful one have you got any questions you want to ask me so we can close this chapter off and move forward?" "I just have one question to ask and one thing to say!" "You said before that I almost complete you? What is it they you need to be completed or what can I do to try to complete and make you whole?" Only two things marry me and have my children!" "What I need to say is that I'm sorry and embarrassed for not waiting for you, I really thought I was just a summer fling to you another conquest for you to chalk up to the experience or that you was hiding a secret wife and family overseas and trying to live more than one lifestyle and I know that I was wrong and all I can say is I'm sorry! "My beautiful one your thought's couldn't have been further from the truth, there wasn't a moment of any day that you wasn't in my thoughts and missing what we had built together in the four weeks of our summer romance were the most beautiful and most gratifying four weeks or my life. Knowing now that because of my job I nearly lost what we had together, but more importantly I nearly lost you Angel and I promise that will never ever happen again.

I know you love me Angel but I just have one question that has played on my mind since I've been back in town? "Yes Mr Dynamite what do you want to know?" "Since you and I have been together I pray that I'm the only one that has had the pleasure of making love to you and that I'm the only man that has touched your pure virgin body?" Angel I need to be assured that I'm the only one that has touched what belongs to me? I really need to know, these thoughts have eaten away at me for months!

"Zane how you can put this question to me, I really don't deserve this question, you left me without a trace or even a word, not even a goodbye." This was never about me it was always about you and why you left me with no contact nothing from you. "So you have been with another man?" "I never said that!" but if I had been I don't believe it's any of your concern. "We both agreed Angel to clear out our skeletons and start fresh, no lies, no secrets." "This is so hard Zane, I never expected this and I certainly didn't expect you to come back!" You're right though there is something you need to know and I'm not sure how you will feel about me after I tell you. Let alone if you will still love me, you do need to be told the truth though if there is any kind of chance of us having a future together. "Angel nothing you could tell me would alter the way I feel about you, "I love you." So tell me Angel what it is. "Well here goes nothing, I have been with another man but believe me there was nothing in it. It was just a one night thing and I also know it would never happen again." I mainly let it happen because I was so fucking angry with you for just up and leaving me the way you did without even so much as a goodbye. I was feeling lonely, vulnerable and I guess thinking about you every spare minute of the day and believe me you consumed my thought process every day, I got as horny as hell and he was there at the right time, and that's pretty much all there is to it. "Angel what's his name?" "I really don't know and that is the honest truth, we never exchanged names and for god sake we never even spoke, we didn't even hold a conversation with each other." "How did this happen then; did you pick him up from the street?' "No I met him at a club!" "What club?" "I met him at my club; actually I should say mine and Braxton's club." "Nightlights." "No!" "Well which fucking club?" what happened to Nightlights, has it been sold, is it not doing very well, what?" "Nightlights is fine in fact it's a goldmine, I'm talking about our other club, our new one!" "What new club?" "We've just built it a few months ago." "Where is it and what's it called?" "It's at our warehouse down the back laneway behind Nightlights and it's called Knickerbox." "What kind of fucked up name is that?" "It's named for its purpose, it was Braxton's idea," If I tell you I know even if you don't hate me you will be very disappointed in me. "I could never hate you baby that's what all this getting our secrets out in the open is all about!" "It's a sex club!" "What in fucking god blazes possessed you to open up a sex club?" "It was originally Braxton's idea but after he explained it all to me and assured me about the clientele need out there for a place like this I didn't need much convincing." "What is this sex club for?" "It's for exclusive clientele that want to be able to let go of their inhibitions and act out their ideal fantasies." "What kind of things?" "We have a sex arena for orgies, swingers, partner swapping a peep show which is set on a timer and charged at extra costing to the admission; with the peep show they get a certain amount of time and when their time is running or run out they have to put more money in the meter, bit similar to a parking meter and mind you this has turned out to be a big money earner, there are private rooms for the more secretive or private clients and then there is our most favourable and popular amongst the clients is the Dungeon (I'm sure I don't have to go into details as to what that is used for)? "Yes, yes I get what that is used for!" there is a fully licensed bar which the clients are served by topless wait staff, a pole for pole dancing, a pornographic movie theatre and a storage / costume room full of wigs, whips, chains, costumes, leather gear, lubricants, massage oils, every imaginable type of condom and an enormous assortment of sex toys. "Aren't you worried about all the weirdos out in this world?" "No all our clients are stringently checked and their names and details are processed fully by police checks and fingerprint evidence to show they don't have a criminal past or current criminal history. They have to succumb to severe and radical medical checks and have to show and supply an updated medical history every three months. "How is this business doing?" we have only been open a couple of months, we're open from Sunday through to Thursday and the club is packing the members in. we made our targets on our opening night and we get so busy we have to turn clients away. I tell you Zane this is really a brainstorm that Braxton came up with and a very hefty nest egg.

So is this where you fucked some other unknown guy? Zane don't say it like that you're making me out to be some kind of slut and I'm not! "I was true to you and I never even thought about being with anyone else when I was away." "Well, Mr Cocksure of himself I was always expecting to be faithful to you, but for how long. I had no idea where you were, how long you were going, for or even if you had intentions of coming back home." "I have explained myself about why I was away and why I couldn't tell you!" "I know that now but back then I had no clue." If you must really know also while I was fucking this guy (as you so blatantly put it) I was imagining it was you and thinking about you the whole time. "Yes" my eyes were closed the whole time and I imagined it was you that was fucking me the whole time, like only you know how to and to fulfil my needs." "When exactly did this happen?" It was on opening night I was there checking out the place and seeing what kind of crowd and types of clientele we would bring in and he was standing near the bar and just walked up to me and asked me if I was interested in testing out my new business. Honestly I was lonely, I felt betrayed by you I was feeling unloved the spice in the atmosphere was raunchy it got me very heated and horny, I didn't feel sexy at all and this guy seemed to show an interest in me, he asked me if I wanted to go to the arena and I said no. he led me to a private room he fucked my brains out and that was it end of story. "Did you like him fucking you?" "Yes I suppose I did, but it was nothing like I have or had with you, it was just sex nothing more; with you my heart races, my body trembles and tingles all over and my sex aches and pulsates." "It is real with you Zane." "Have you got any desire to go back there in a sexual fashion?" "No definitely not!" "May I ask why not?" "Because all it was Zane was a fantasy, and I'm not a fantasy kind of girl, I'm a marriage with a white wedding dress and veil and a house with the picket fence and a baby in the carriage kind of girl." The next day after I woke up I realised I had made a big mistake and I made a vow then that to me all Knickerbox was just a business venture; a very lucrative one may I add but just a business. "Would you go there with me?" Zane I would go to the moon and back with you, but why would you want to go there when you have your place and I have my house? "I want to see how hot and horny you get when you're at this club and to see how far to the edge I can push you to the brink!" I can see how hot and horny you're getting now with me just talking about with you my beautiful one, and I bet your pussy is very moist as well isn't it? "Yes I'm hot, sexy, horny and wet but you do that to me on any given day and in any place." 'Can I take you there and fuck the arse off you and show you how much I love you and let everyone know that you are mine and belong only to me?" You are all mine, have you got that? Have I made myself clear? "Aye Captain I only wants you and I don't want to belong to anyone else." "So you will let me take you to Knickerbox?" "I will but only on one condition?" "My beautiful one what condition would that be?" "We go on a night when were closed and we have the whole place to ourselves." "I think I can go along with that idea." "Is our secret telling time over with now?" "Yes, my beautiful one but I just have one more final question to ask you." "Oh and what's that?" "What roles do you and Braxton play in this business?" "Mr Dynamite to answer your question I handle all the books and accounts and I also do some of the bookings that come in through our website." Braxton is in charge of all the day to day stuff that goes into the business for example he orders all the stock, the deliveries, merchandise inventories, cash flow our staff including the cleaners, and does all the screening of the clients and most of the bookings and keeping all our bookings, website and records up to date.

Jett is in charge of all the building and site works and maintenance. So you can see my role in the business is very minimal. Is that what you wanted to hear? "Yes, and all I want is to get you back in my arms, naked and make the most passionate love to you that I guarantee you would ever have experienced, and believe me you will be begging for more." "Really please, Zane take me and do to me what you must, I can't wait." "I love you Angel my beautiful one!" "I love you to Mr Dynamite Zane Channing!"

15

Investigation

*B*lake rings Zane to tell him more threatening letters have turned up, the more letters, that arrived the more threatening they became.

"Blake what have you come up with?" We have to catch this son of a bitch I'm sick of this mother fucker's threats! I know one thing is for sure I definitely can't take Angel back there it definitely isn't safe.

"No definitely Zane, stay put." I will fax you copies of the letters and letting you know we're still waiting for the forensics to come back to see if any fingerprints have been left on any of the letters and identifiable. One though Zane we're positive this has not been done Rogue Tyler. He could be the reason behind the letters but not actually involved.

"What is your theory with all the letters and information you have already?" "Blake we are missing the link between Rogue Tyler and his financial crisis, someone must be feeding money to Rogue and that someone must be holding his finances and debts over his head and possibly even be using their funds for collateral against him."

When Angel had taken on his books and then took them to Storm Mason tells me that one, she has stepped on someone's territory and two, was too close to they didn't want anyone else to know. My guess it is a front for something else, perhaps drugs, fraud or maybe even money laundering. My guess is that whoever it is using Rogue Tyler's auto shop as a front for their criminal activities, and at a rough guess Rogue is either scared shitless and keeping out of everyone's way or he is so hooked on his eccentric lifestyle and such a dumb arse prick he is oblivious to what is going on around him. "We all agree with that Zane with our observations Rogue is either too drunk, hooked up with different sheilas every night and too stupid to be plotting this." "I guess the million dollar question is, what are they running through the shop, and who is it?"

"Can you get into the auto shop over night to plant some cameras and hearing devices in there?" "Yes most certainly can, I will organise that as soon as I get off the phone to you!" "If we can get the surveillance devices in there we can see and hear who is coming and going and what is being said!" "Both Storm and I agree that is the best plan of attack." "Should I get our alarm technicians out there also so they can bypass the alarm system?" "Brilliant idea, yes we need that done, that is a given." Are Wade and his family being looked after? "There is no need to worry about them we have them isolated and covered." I have also put security on the Police Station, on Jett Mark's house on Braxton Miles house and the club. "Good job Blake you've taken all the right steps and put all the right measures in place and now it is time to play cat and mouse."

Tonight I'm going to go over all the evidence again and look over the letters and make sure there is nothing we have missed or over looked, and then if I come up with anything then I will call you straight back. Meanwhile contact me as soon as possible if you come up with anything else? "Sure will Zane take care and look after that gorgeous woman of yours?" "I will and let it be noted no one will get near my woman!"

Zane and Angel retire for the night, their kissing passionately and Zane is running his fingers through her hair, Angel runs her fingers down his back, around his neck along his face, through his hair and everywhere else you can touch someone. Zane lifts Angel's top off over head and pulls her pants down and off and throws them to the floor, he gently lifts her up and lays her across the bed, Angel undresses Zane and they are caressing each other naked on the bed. "Mr Dynamite this is what I remember and how I remember us to be and I never want to lose or change what we have." "My beautiful one I have never forgotten the thoughts of us and every day I get a whole picture of new thoughts about us, who we are as a couple, the love and romantic passion we share and mostly I have realised to never take any day for granted." My thoughts are so constant every day that they punish my brain, the guilt I carry around knowing that my egotistical, male macho pride nearly lost the one thing in life that I not only love the most and care about, but that I also could have missed out on for ever if I had lost you." Thinking about us and what we shared is a constant and was the only thing that put me to sleep at night, you're a sleeping tranquiliser one minute and then you have the reverse effect on me the next like I'm hooked on Ritalin and can't stop from wanting and needing you. Never could I have enough of you or ever tire of you; you are the bounce in my ball, (literally). Everything I think about and every thought that transcribes in my head tell me that the only important thing that matters in my life is you Angel my beautiful one, and I promise you will never want for anything and I will be both true and faithful throughout our eternal lives. There is one thing you must realise though is that as much as it would be perfect we can't stay here forever, we do need to go back home for family, friends and our work commitments, but until we catch that bastard this is our home.

If you want though my beautiful one we can relocate you back here permanently or you can quit and stay home and enjoy me cherishing you and spoiling you, or I could incorporate a role in the company for you to work alongside me. "Baby it is your call." I do vow though Angel to always protect you and keep you out of harm's way. "Is there any news in regards to this matter yet?" "No but I do feel a breakthrough at any moment." Now can we stop yapping and get down to what we do best and what really matters, you sexy hot woman I just can't get enough of you. Angel I want you right now, look how big and hard my cock is for your very hungry pussy, this is because of the effect you have on me. "Mr Dynamite I'm, wet, moist and horny and I want you just as bad, and I sir can't ever get enough of you either."

Zane starts kissing Angel around the neck, her back down her spine and down along the back of her legs in between her legs through her triangle pubic hair that sat so neatly trimmed across the top of her pussy making her sex very visible indeed. She always seems to have just the right amount of pubic hair on the top of her mound. Running his fingers down her back, spine backs of legs and between her legs is always a sensation for Angel sending tingling sensations beaming through her body. Her nipples are a soft brown colour 'and they are so erect, taut and well positioned (the perfect size for breastfeeding our kids) says Zane, and just the right hand and mouth size. The more Zane rubbed pulled, licked, fondled and teased the nipple between his fingers with such intent and passion the more erect and standing to attention they became, the more frenzied, excited and titillated Angel got. The intensity from Zane had Angel writhing and squirming underneath trapped but not wanting to be free.

Passion of desire burning through Angel's body made Zane harder and hornier, he loved to watch her squirm with desire and teeter on the brink following orgasm after orgasm, and he kept pushing her harder and harder to the extreme maximum of climatic orgasms and Angel knew no one else could satisfy and fulfil her needs or make her come to dynamic overloads like her Mr Dynamite.

Angel starts kissing and nibbling at his ears, his face and around his neck he is shaking with the sense of her warm breath running down his spine then their lips met for one almighty passionate kiss with their tongues, rhythm for rhythm tonguing deep down the back of each other's throats. Suddenly Zane pulls away and moves down the bed lower, parts Angel's legs throws them both high over his shoulders and lashes her sweet sex with such force and intensity, he licks her pussy lobes until Angel is moaning and thrashing around underneath him and nearly falling off the edge of the bed. Zane runs his tongue along her clitoris and pushes his tongue deep inside her beautiful wet pussy; she's on the verge of exploding, her orgasm intensifying. He is relentless, he sucks and chews on her flaps then Angel gets this feeling a sharp point is pressing inside her. Zane has thrust two fingers deep inside her sex; she is on the edge gripping his back so tight she wonders if she has left scratches or finger indents on his skin. Then out of nowhere a third finger penetrates her, she is screaming, moaning pleading for his release to relinquish the emotional satisfaction he has on her pleading with him to stop, she can't take anymore, she is exploding, numb intoxicated with both pleasure and the most joyous pain that is so intense it hurts.

Zane pulls out his fingers and himself almost on the brink of orgasm, sticks his cock deep inside Angel's tunnel of love, oh my god my beautiful one I'm that horny just through you and your orgasms that I'm going to shoot you full of my love seed, oh baby one more thrust and I'm there with you and Angel pushes back deep onto his penetrating rod that's boring inside of her like a drill in a mine shaft and with that he shoots his release and fills her pussy with another load of his hot spunk inside her love box. He slowly pulls his semi erect cock out of her and rolls on the bed alongside her and wrapping her in his arms. "Was that up to your expectations my beautiful one?" "You're always up to my expectations, every time taking me that little bit further, you how to take me to our magical place." "I hope I'm the one and the only ever to take you in your life." "Of course, your enough for me, how many times do I have to try to reassure you that I don't want or need anyone else, I have a hard enough time keeping up with you.' you always take me to the edge and leave me fulfilled, numb, exhausted, completely satisfied and the feeling you leave me is indescribable. Angel lay in his arms staring up at the ceiling. "Angel what's wrong, what is on your mind, is it anything I have done or said?" "No Zane of course not, nothing could be more further from the truth." 'Then talk to me." 'No I was just thinking, but everything is good in fact better than good!" Angel we made a promise to not hold anything back or keep secrets from each other, now tell me what's bothering you? "It's more to the point of something I want." "Anything Angel I will give you anything you want or need." "Really and you won't pass judgement on me. Now you know me Angel and you know that, that would never happen!" "I was just wondering how you would feel about anal sex?" "I'm definitely all for it with a willing partner." What are you saying my beautiful one you want to try it? "Um, no I want to be able to receive it and incorporate it into our sexual escapades." "So have you tried anal sex before?" "Yes." "When and with who?" "Does it really matter?" "It does if we are serious about not sharing everything and having secrets then yes it does matter!" 'It was the opening night at Knickerbox with that unknown guy he introduced me to it and I really enjoyed it." "Did you ride bareback?" "No definitely not!" "What about me?" "Do you ride bare back now?" "Yes and you and I both love it!" "Then there is your answer." "Angel my beautiful one I'm your magical genie and your wish is my command, and just letting you know I'm a very lucky man." They both drifted off into a solid sleep.

The next morning while Angel slept peacefully, Zane got up and went over all the information, suspects, lists and motives and all the evidence that had been gathered for him by Blake, Storm and the entire force. He is pulling his hair out that they haven't come across a simple solitary lead, to put them in reach of catching this bastard. Frustrated he looks over the evidence once again and checks the financial and bank statements. That's interesting said Zane; why didn't any of us pick this up earlier? Where are those internet transfers coming from, and more so from who? Zane curiously then enters the bank account digits into his computer and bang he struck a match. It is coming from a Robert Mullins and Zane enters his name into the police criminal files data base and there is the connection. Step brother of one Rogue Tyler and his criminal history is extensive; his record is as long as his arm with offences ranging from fourteen till now. His offences range from grand larceny, armed holdups, drug dealing, assault, embezzlement and fraud, kidnapping, money laundering and murder. "Well, well Mr Robert Mullins I've got you now "you son of a bitch".

"With the new information he immediately phones Blake with his findings."

16

The Break Through

Blake you need to organise a full surveillance on Robert Mullins, lay low though and don't let him know we're on to him. We can't arrest him or catch him until we have something on camera or can catch him in the act. So for the time being we watch every move this cunning slippery little sucker does, monitor every call that comes in and out of his phone and watch every move he makes. We need to put taps on both his and Rogue Tyler's phones. "Zane what's your take on this?" "I think Rogue's elaborate and eccentric lifestyle had caught up with him, along comes the evil stepbrother who has somehow blackmailed Rogue into covering his arse through the automotive shop." I would bet he's dealing in drugs, fraud and embezzlement and being the master fraudster and embezzler is using the auto shop to front his criminal activities and the profits from the money is fronting Rogue's finances and his compulsive spending.

"Blake gets the guys together to set up the surveillance and he calls their communications team to get into both their houses and businesses to put taps on their phones and hide cameras around the properties everywhere."

"Storm Mason Police Sergeant organises the man power to step up the surveillance so they can catch the bastard that is holding the locals of Auburn Creek fearful for their lives. Robert Mullins lives only ten minutes away from Auburn Creek in Goulburn Forest.

Zane puts a trace and tracking device on all Robert Mullins and Rogue Tyler's bank transactions. They're all watching their transactions like Hawkeyes and just waiting for that one invalid unauthorised payment to come through then they has got him.

"Zane's team manage to get inside the auto shop and they set the cameras and phone taps up ready to go. After an all-night surveillance they followed Rogue from the local club, noting how much he had spent and gambled and staggered to an unknown female persons house who they know Rogue had been cavorting at the club with all night, staggered back to her house accompanied with the unknown female drunk and oblivious to the surroundings around him. Setting up Rogue's house and work was quite an easy task for them to pull off. "Blake have you got the all clear to get into Robert's house?" 'Zane it is all clear and the technicians are hear as we speak."

"Good it won't be long now before we catch that fucking son of a bitch!"

Two weeks later they gather all their information, listen to the recordings from the tapped phones and view the footage recorded on the hidden cameras.

"Right boys I'm staying put to watch Angel, but you all go and make the arrest and bring them into the station in custody and charge them and read them their right's and throw the fucking book at them and then transfer them both to headquarters here in Sydney."

"Blake when you get them at headquarters call me and I will meet you there." I want to confront these bastards and then I know they will both be dealt with and then Angel will be safe.

17

Closing In

In an early morning raid the cops make the jump on both Rogue Tyler's house and Robert Mullin's houses and too their shock, both had escaped and were nowhere to be found. "Fuck someone must've tipped them off, now who is going to break the news to Zane?" asks Blake? The team votes Blake to do the honours seems he is in charge of leading the team into catching these bastards. "Geez I'm going to be hung out to dry and shot the moment Zane gets wind of this." How the fuck could you useless fucking incompetent idiots fuck this up? Blake screams out! What fucking went wrong? Right at that moment Blake receives a call from one of the men in their team: Blake we're in Robert's house and to our dismay the bastard must've figured out we were onto him, he has cut the surveillance cameras and removed the bugs from his phones. We did a mobile check and it looks as though he now has a disposable phone which we can't trace. Robert has only taken minimal things in a backpack style bag, he has taken a few items of clothing, his wallet, bank books and bank statements and his passport and his revolver. It looks like everything else has been left behind. "Any sign of Rogue?" "No but I don't think he has gone far, there doesn't seem to be anything touched or missing, so our guess is that he is just laying low somewhere probably drunk and sleeping it off at some sheilas place." Most likely that sheila he has been cavorting at the club with lately would be our bet. "Focus on Rogue, and then maybe he will lead us to his step brother!" "Zane hi it's me Blake I have an update for you but I don't think you're going to be happy with what I have to tell you." "Well for fuck sake Blake spit it out, what the fucking hell are you telling me?" "We followed protocol and acted on you and Storm's orders and raided at five thirty am as you ordered but neither we're there at their houses, I'm afraid we have lost them." What the fucking hell do you mean you have lost them?" "Robert cut the surveillance cameras, took the bugs out of the phones and has replaced his mobile with a disposable untraceable one!" he only has a small back pack of stuff with him and has left his car behind so that tells us he has fled on foot in a hurry.

"How the fuck did you clowns manage to fuck this up?" Blake we have found spies and terrorists in the Middle East and you can't find a fucking common conman criminal. My training must be slipping. If you were all surrounded and surveying his house then how the fuck did he slip past you all? "We found an underground tunnel under his bedroom floor and runs under his back yard and out onto the alley way past his back fence." That is the only logical explanation we can come up with, and the only possibility that could have gotten him past us. "What about Rogue, or have you lost him to?" "No we don't have him either but nothing is gone or untouched so we're assuming he is just crashed out drunk somewhere and I have put all available patrols into looking and capturing him and hopefully he will lead us to the arrest of Robert fucking Mullins." "Do not fucking stand there telling me about it, just get your arses out there and catch the bastards and God help the lot of you if anything happens to Angel, Wade or his family, I swear to god I won't be responsible for my actions." Now get to work and don't contact me till your have something positive to tell me!" Blake sharp up and toughen the guys in our team and on the force, for fuck's sake!' "Consider it done Zane, and don't worry we will get them."

18

Madison Carter

adison Carter was the local personal trainer and gym owner and instructor in Auburn Grove, Maddie as she likes to be called is Angel Hart's best friend and confidant, having befriended her and Jett after they arrived in Auburn Grove and they have been besties ever since.

"Maddie is Jett's personal trainer and his long-time girlfriend and is also is Angel's personal trainer and the three of them train up to three times a week, except gym junkie Maddie who runs a minimum of twenty kilometres every day and trains religiously every day. Although Maddie and Jett have tried to hide their romance from everyone else all of Auburn Grove suspect that they are an item and whispers and rumours down the street seem to indicate the same thing.

"Angel has never been able to comprehend why they just won't come out and admit they are a couple, but says with her complacent reply 'oh well each to their own I suppose'." Watching them together though is like watching a candle to a spark its explosive.

Maddie rings Angel on her mobile, hi Angel it's me Maddie where are you." I haven't seen anything of you or heard from you in weeks is everything ok?

"Zane is telling Angel in the background not to give any information away." "Hi Maddie how are you?" I'm okay I just wanted to get away for a while to sort myself out and take some time out from work and the club. I asked Wade if I could take some of my leave that was owing to me and go away for a while and he approved it, so that's what I did. I'm sorry I didn't give you a call and tell you I guess it just happened so quick that I didn't give it another thought. "Well why didn't you talk to me? You know I'm a good listener." I wasn't even aware that you were going through anything that you needed to get away from except for pining for that bloody Zane Channing. Angel honestly you really need to put him and that part of your past behind you and move forward. Where are you staying? "I'm in the city." Angel can I come up and visit you for a few days? Angel pauses for a moment and looks over at Zane for a signal. Maddie that would be great!. When are you thinking of coming? "I will drive up on Friday, if that is okay?" "Great I will text you the address and the details how to find it." Also Maddie can you please do me a favour? "Yes, Angel anything, what would you like me to do?" "Can you please travel up with Jett?" "Of course, but I do know he is flat out at work but I will tell him." "Please Maddie I can't explain now but I will let you both know when you get here, so can you tell him I need to see him urgently." One more thing Maddie you have to promise me that you and Jett will not mention anything to anyone about me being away or where I am, and better still please don't even let on to anyone that you have even spoken to me on the phone. "Please Maddie I need you to promise." "I promise Angel but your scaring me, what's going on?" "Just trust me Maddie please! I can't go into it now over the phone." "You have my word Angel; I will see you before lunch on Friday with Jett." "Bye" "Bye Maddie."

Madison Carter has hair the colour of ebony, blue green eyes a tall slim physique even though her body is thick set like that of an athlete and she has a thirty six A inch bust, and she is mighty proud of her bust size as are the males that swoon and whistle at her when they watch her walk down the street or when they see her at the gym. She loves the whistles and stares that she receives on an almost daily basis and loves to be the centre of attention. A solid gym junkie and devout vegan Maddie works tirelessly and puts her body through an extreme workout regime seven days per week so she can continuously keep her body in tip top shape. "Madison Carter was born and bred in Auburn Creek to a wealthy family, her father Johnathon is the town's local dentist and her mum Katherine is the local school principal. An only child Maddie is used to getting whatever she wanted. Worlds apart from the family and childhood Angel and Jett had and unlike Maddie who never wanted for a thing. For her eighteenth birthday her parent's brought her a red BMW convertible, and for her twenty first birthdays they purchased the local gym and fitness training centre from the previous owner Craig Radcliffe. Craig wanted to pursue new interests including sail around the world and needed to sell the fitness centre to pay for his luxury boat and finance his travel. Maddie takes a stroll over to the mega plaza to tell her boyfriend Jett he needs to accompany her to Sydney to meet up with Angel. "Hi honey, what brings you over here?" I spoke to Angel today and I'm telling you there is something weird going on with her. Did you know that she is on personal time in the city and she has been gone for weeks? "Jesus Christ honey, I've been so busy working I didn't realise how long since visits with her or even when I last spoke to her." Fuck that is weird that she never told me she was going; she generally tells me everything. "That is what I'm trying to tell you and she told me to bring you because she needed to speak with you urgently and she was so vague while she was talking to me, almost like someone was coaching her on what to say." Another thing she said to me was we were to tell no one I made contact with her and spoke to her on the phone and that we couldn't tell anyone where she was or that we had heard from her and especially that no one must know she is in Sydney. "This is so not like my sister!" Normally I would say that I was too busy to leave here but considering the circumstances I'm going with you! My boys can handle a few days or so without me. "Jett we will travel up in my car and I thought we would leave by about eight am, then that way we will arrive there by lunch time." "That's cool, I'm all for that." Friday it is! We will both be ready so don't go fluffing about and stressing, I'm sure everything will be fine. Thanks honey, for letting me know I really appreciate it. If you hadn't said anything to me I hate to realise how long it would have been between communications there had been between Angel and me.

Friday finally comes around and Jett and Maddie pack up the car and Maddie being the perfectionist that she is has to load the car her way. Jett throws his bag in the boot and then they set off a little before eight am, for the three hour drive to Sydney city. Eleven thirty and Maddie and Jett arrive at the address that Angel had texted Madison. "Wholly fuck, Jett I thought my folks house was a mansion, this is a fucking palace!" I wonder how Angel got onto this place Maddie asks Jett with a hint of curiosity? "Fuck I didn't even know these kinds of houses even existed except in Beverly Hills!" "Well this has certainly changed that thought process." "Wow Angel has definitely stepped up the ante." 'You got that bloody right." "But how, I can't fathom this or work it out?" Angel has become so secretive, which is so unlike her. Maddie drives the long path to the house expecting to be greeted by Angel, only to find two guys with guns, and uniforms signalling Maddie to drive to the back of the house. The two guys collect their bags and escort them to the back door, and they both walk into the big living area to be greeted by Angel. "Hi guys thanks for coming, I really appreciate it." "Angel what the fuck is going on?" whose house is this? And what the fuck are you doing here?

"Angel you haven't said anything to me your best friend." "Don't worry about best friend, what about your brother?" while Angel is now lost for words and trying to work out how she is going to tell them what's happened, Zane steps in to save the day for her yet again. "Hello guys, thanks for coming; it really means a lot to Angel and to me too." I personally think this is just what Angel needed! "Well Mr fucking Channing what have you done to Angel?" Did you kidnap her and now you're holding her captive? Gripes Maddie. "Angel I thought you was moving on from this low life?" "Jett, Maddie please stop!" "It's okay my beautiful one, I will fill them in and make them listen and understand." Firstly guys I couldn't tell Angel about my other life. Maddie jumps in, 'you're fucking married aren't you?' I knew it! "No I'm not married and there is no other woman and I won't nor will I ever want another woman but Angel, she has my heart and my soul." Guys please sit down. Over the summer I was called away on a secret mission. "Are you telling us you're a kind of spy like James Bond?" "Something like that I'm a Special Forces agent and a private investigator." I spend a lot of time in war torn countries mainly the Middle East and as I was on top secret missions I couldn't tell Angel what I was doing or that I had to go away. I hadn't been back from the Middle East long when I got a call from Storm Mason. "Storm, why the fuck would he be calling from back home to you?""

Jett, Angel was handling Rogue Tyler's books for his business and his personal books, and with working out all his figures she realised that his books didn't add up, so she took them to Storm to tell him her findings." Storm looked at them and believed that they warranted an investigation. Only before we could even have a look at them Angel and Wade had been sent anonymously threatening letters. So we as a team decided to send Wade and his family away under my companies protection and I was not prepared to leave Angel behind where she was a target so I insisted she come away to stay here with me where I could watch her twenty four seven, that is why it was so important she didn't contact you both or why it was necessary that neither of you told anyone where she was. "Zane I, I mean we are both sorry for the way we carried on to you and I want to say thanks for looking after my sister, she is the only family I have or that we both consider family." Zane, thanks from me also for taking care of my best friend Angel is not only my best friend she is the sister I never had."

"You're both welcome and as you can see all my energy is being put into keeping my beautiful one safe and out of harm's way."

Thank god now we've got that all out the way and in the open, now check everything is in order in your room and come down and do what you came here to do in the first place. "To, visit with Angel."

"Well first things first can we go for a swim in the Palace pool, asks Maddie?" "Of course, what say we all go for a swim says Zane?" "But I don't have any swim wear professes Angel! "Well my beautiful I'm fine with that, do you see me complaining?" "Zane I can't swim naked my brother is here!" "I'm just joking, there are all sorts of bathers and bikinis in the pool room dresser." "Woo hoo yells, out Maddie."

In less than five minutes they're all in the pool swimming, laughing, each couple kissing and cuddling and Zane summons his kitchen staff to bring out drinks and nibbles to the pool area. Sitting around the pool area relaxing after their swim they were all seated and talking about their pasts and telling Zane how they all became to being connected. "Zane says Jett thanks for looking after my sister, I had no idea that she was even anything going on!" I guess I have been so self-absorbed with my workload and Maddie that I didn't even give Angel another thought, and I certainly wouldn't have been able to live with myself if anything had happened to her." "Angel next time promise me you will come to me after all that's what best friends are for?"

"I'm sorry guys but I was so scared I didn't want to drag anyone else through this." "Sorry guys but Angel did the right thing not telling you both or anyone else for that matter." She had to make sure she kept within her boundaries to protect everyone especially herself and Wade and his family.

"Are you going to catch those sons of bitches Zane?" 'You bet your bottom dollar I'm going to catch both those mother fucker's and beat the fucking shit out of both of them myself. "Count me in!" "Thanks Jett but between Blake Storm, myself and the troops we have this covered, but thanks anyway for the offer." You will help us by looking after Madison. "Oh I guarantee Zane and you have my word, I will definitely look after Maddie, I don't know what I would do without her!"

"Zane I don't mean to be blunt and forward but my parents are very wealthy, in fact one of the wealthiest families in Auburn Creek and not even with their wealth could they live up to your expectations and wealth, but if you don't mind me asking, how can you afford pure luxury like this when everyone knows the Special Forces and private Investigation business still wouldn't amount to this kind of lifestyle and opulence?"

To put your mind at ease Maddie my family are the Fishers Generation. One in the Same Fishers family that owned the majority of the land in Auburn Creek. My Great Grandparents owned the first jewellery store, and my great grand dad was the local blacksmith. Then they went into developing all the land they owned and turned them into residential housing, commercial businesses and manufacturing factories. Then my grandparents took over from them and from there, my family inherited the lot. My parents gave me a majority of my inheritance when I turned twenty one and with my inheritance and the money I had saved from working overseas I brought all this land and an old house that was on the property. Four years ago I knocked the house down and built this one. "Did your family by any chance adopt out another son (Jett asks)?" Everyone all laughs in unison. "Angel you have it made dear friend, a gorgeous man that you can clearly see adores you and a big palace and more money than the Queen!" "Maddie I'm not after Zane's money or house, you should know me better than that!" 'Angel what is mine is all yours." "Thanks Mr Dynamite but I'm not in this for the money or the wealth." "So what are you saying?" Do you want me to give away all our money and walk away from this house? "No that is not what I'm saying!" Look can we just change the subject? "Okay Done!"

They spent the rest of the weekend playing tennis, walking along the beach, swimming, drinking and laughing. Sunday late afternoon came and Jett and Maddie loaded up the car ready for their three hour drive back to sleepy Auburn Creek.

19

Braxton Finds Love

Braxton has run himself into the ground running both Nightlights and Knickerbox covering for Angel while she is on extended leave.

"Fuck how am I supposed to answer my inhibitions and make full use of my own sex club when I haven't even got five seconds to scratch myself?" Surely Angel must be coming back soon! Scott the head barman at Nightlights asks Braxton when Angel is coming back. "You tell me and we will both fucking know snaps Braxton." I do know one thing though I can't hold down the fort much longer here on my own without a day off. "Boss I think you should ring her!" "The whole idea of this trip though was to get away and take some time out, not have me ringing and harassing her." "True but you didn't think she would be gone for a month a more." "Yes I know that's true and I have already decided that I'm going to have to put on more staff and maybe a couple of extra managers on a rotation basis to give me a day or two off, and the business is increasing so much all the time much quicker than we ever anticipated so we really do need to hire extra staff for the two clubs." I will give her another week and then I will give her a call. Braxton steps out the back to catch up on the entire inventory and order stock that needs to be bought in and stocked up. he then gets on the computer and pays all the past due and due now accounts, he does the payroll, pulls out the deliveries and orders folders and starts ticking of what needs to be ordered, what is to be picked up and what gets delivered. Braxton then counts out the day's takings, rolls it up into an elastic band and puts it into a plastic money bag, which will then go into the large calico money bag. He then enters the code for the safe and adds it in with the rest of the week's takings and has it ready for the armguards security trucks to pick up on Friday afternoon. Braxton then does the daily takings in the accounts book and loads them the total amounts into the computer data base.

"Fuck without even adding Knickerbox our takings are up seventy percent." Shit this really is setting Angel and me up financially for our futures, and without doing any figures for today and judging by the looks of the bookings and the crowds that are going to be coming through our doors tonight I think I can safely say were killing it." (Braxton says to himself) I knew in my heart this is what I was meant to do and with Angel as my business partner we make an unbeatable team, I can see myself laying back on a tropical island basking in the sun sipping on Pina-coladas, and boasting about my millionaire lifestyle. Bathing in my glory and all the hard work we have put into these businesses I can definitely feel my black sports car coming in the not too far future. From the back office Braxton dials 717on the internal line that runs directly through to Knickerbox, hi Marcus it's Braxton?; I need the inventory, the stocks and deliveries folder and the total weekly takings including todays amounts sent over to me please immediately with Jimmy James. "Not a problem boss I'm only too willing to help you out I will get on it right away and send him over with them." Is there anything else I can help you out with while I'm at it and on the phone to you?" "No but I'm curiously wondering how things are in the guests department for tonight and what was the rest of the week like?" "Boss was up an average of ten percent every night and tonight has been the busiest yet to date, but without an actual calculator in front of me, I would guess our profits in total would be up by at least seventy percent and could even be hitting as high as eighty percent." "Fuck man that is wicked, insane but incredible especially in these hard economic times and it just goes to show Marcus no matter how bad the economy or how much unemployment is out there, there is no price on love or sex or stopping people, from drinking, dancing and out having a good time." "You have that right boss; the more clients we have using the club, the more word of mouth is getting out the busier we keep on getting." "Good job mate, keep up the good work, I'm in the process of making you the Manager in charge of Knickerbox so just bear with me till Angel gets back and keep the rest of the staff members at the top of their game." We really can't afford to lose our reputation we have built up in so short of time." Goodnight Marcus, and send Jimmy James with the paper work immediately.

Jimmy James is the clubs main security guard, bouncer and he came recommended to us and screened from Fisher Security, he takes risks with both the drunken clients any loiters or under aged drinkers, and with the handlings of the clubs takings to ensure its safety to arrive from Knickerbox to Nightlights safe. He is a bit of a laugh around the clubs because of his parent's lack of originality in his birth name.

A true Irishman at heart his parents named him after both his grandfather's. One was named Jimmy O'Leary and the other was James Flaherty, so his genius parents combined the two. His parents father Harry and mother Mary, Jimmy and his seven other siblings moved out to Australia when Jimmy was ten years old from Ireland that was twenty five years ago, but with the strength of his Irish accent you would swear it was only yesterday. Jimmy was with us from the start of our Night lights opening and has been with us ever since. Jimmy looks like the kind of guy that butter wouldn't melt in his mouth but with a height of one hundred and eighty three centimetres, fire engine red hair, hazel eyes and muscles as big as Mohammed he is not the kind of guy you want to mess around with. Never though could you find a more loyal, obligated and trusting employee and Jimmy has proven to us that he really is worth his weight in gold.

Five minutes later as regular as clock work there is the distinct Jimmy James knock at the office door, with all the paper work, orders, delivery dockets and instructions and the week's takings. "Thanks Jimmy, you know you're much appreciated here." "Your most welcome boss and you know just to buzz me if you need me for anything else, goodnight."

Finally an hour later Braxton has finished ordering the stock, entering the figures into the data base and adding the takings and putting them into the combination safe and says to himself, on that note I think I will go out to the bar have a quick drink and head home to bed, even though half of him is wishing that the girl who has been coming in every night for the past few weeks drinking with him till the wee hours the next morning is sitting at one of the tables waiting for him.

When Braxton gets out into the bar area she is nowhere to be seen although disappointed but unbelievably tired Braxton comments to him (I guess it was for the best because now I can I can go home and try to get goodnights sleep). Upon saying that an arm is put around his neck and the other arm put on his hand and then she clutched Braxton into a tight embrace. Before Braxton even has a chance to turn around and face her he finds himself being kissed all around his neck and his ear lobes are being nibbled at provocatively and seductively and being tickled by her scintillating mouth and tongue and just the thought of her warm breathe down the back of his neck and back are starting to make him sweat and pant like a hot puppy, the tension that is building up inside him, his hair is starting to spike, his cock is now fully erect and the blood flow to the veins of his cock are pumping blood so fast through his shaft so fast he feels like he is going to come in his pants. He can feel his little nipple buds starting to tingle and his ball sacks are filling up fast with his man seed.

Braxton spins around on the bar stool and meets his lips with hers, he kisses her passionately and runs his tongue along her luscious lips and around her mouth and then sticks his tongue in her mouth as far as it will go. She reciprocates his every move tonguing his mouth, his lips outlining his mouth with her strawberry scented tongue.

Braxton kisses her all around her neck and he now nibbles at her ear lobes and drives her totally insane. He takes a chance and puts his hand up her dress only to find his heart racing and pounding even harder and faster. He realises she isn't wearing any underwear. "Where are your pants he asks?" Did you not wear any here or did you dispose of them just before. "Why are you bothered or worried?" "Hell no you've given biggest hard on in a long time and possibly of all time." "Just between you and me my panties are in my handbag." Braxton lets his fingers find his way around her hairless muff triangle. "Fuck your muffs so soft and smooth!" "Do you like shaved or unshaven, she asks?" "I like them any way but I have to confess your smooth muff is turning me on real bad." Braxton fondles her love triangle rubbing his hand across the top of her sex, he then pulls his hand out from under her dress and licks his fingers to leave saliva on his fingers so he can insert his fingers inside her sex with ease. "Let me tell you something Mr Hotshot I really don't think you needed to wet your fingers, I'm really wet anyway, and in fact I'm so wet my mickey juices are running down the insides of my legs.

With that Braxton sticks first one finger into her warm, tight snatch, he moves his finger deeper inside of her sex and he finds her clitoris and fingers insatiably. Now she starts to rock side to side and moan but oblivious of anyone that may be watching or listening to her moans of pleasure. Braxton fondles her meaty labia flesh and twirls her flaps between his fingers; he knows he is sending her right over the edge. She doesn't care so neither does he, then without any warning he shoves two fingers deep into her vagina; Braxton is fingering her with such vigour and haste. The pressure she is feeling is so intense like a bubble is ready to burst inside of her. "Stop now please or I'm going to scream this club down with my climax."

Well my sexy lady do you want to finish this out the back or come back to my place? "How far is your place, she replies?" "A couple of minutes down the road and even quicker if we run." "Then your place it is!" In no time at all they were both rushing through his front door, with clothes being pulled of each other and thrown around everywhere. Braxton picks up his horny lover and carries her straight to his bedroom and lays her on his bed. Within seconds Braxton is straight in between her legs whipping and lashing at her swollen, ripe pussy flaps, tonguing her clitoris and licking her internally all over the inside of her vagina. All she can do is run her hands through his hair and wriggle and squirm underneath him.

Braxton puts his huge erect shaft and rubs it around her mouth and lips, she obligingly opens her mouth to receive his huge manhood and licks around his cockhead, nibbling at his sensitive organ, then she runs her tongue from top to bottom along his shaft outlining with her tongue the thick veins that protrude on the outside of his man beast. Her hands massage his balls and she fondles them with much vigour and passion. His lover takes his balls in her mouth and sucks like there is no tomorrow. Rolling the balls around in her mouth Braxton is on the verge, never in his wildest dreams has any other woman ever taken his shaft and sperm bags and licked and sucked them like it was going to be their last feed ever. Not in his life has he ever been tortured with fire and passion like she was doing to him now. "Fuck if you don't stop I'm afraid I will have to shoot my load in your mouth and if I do that then you have to swallow every last drop!" "I think I can handle that!"

"Why don't you kneel on all fours and let me fuck you from behind and I guarantee my shaft will be imbedded so deep in your tight love box you will be begging me for mercy!" "I think I will have to put your words and actions to the test." In a split second she was on all fours and Braxton had shoved his fully erect thick elongated cock so deep inside her, she felt her vaginal walls had collapsed. "Did I hurt you my sexy lady?" "No it's just that you penetrated me so deep I thought you had split me in halves." With that he pumped her harder and more agile and fierce, they were both on fire, she throwing herself back hard on every thrust he drove into her.

The more he thrust into her the harder she fucked him back, she could feel the rise in his cock swell inside her as he could feel the tightness of her pussy and the swelling of her vulva. They both knew they both knew their climatic finish was close, their orgasm electrifying, spasmodic and volcanic was ready to spontaneously combust. Both of them on the edge building into frenzy, so sexual and gratifying, so indulgent, his sexy one then gave a god all mighty screech and her pussy pulsated over his throbbing soon to be released cock. The jism building up from his bulls was setting his heart and pulse racing. Braxton could no longer hold back his seed, she writhed and wriggled and that was enough to set him off like a volcanic eruption, his seed well erupted in her much fucked moist pussy. Delirious, numb, weak and speechless they both just lay on the bed looking into each other's eyes. The eyes told the story, Braxton wanted love now on a permanent basis and his sexy one came to the club to find him. Finally after their heart rate and pulses had slowed back down to normal and they both took deep breaths they could at last find the energy to talk.

"I don't know your name but one thing is perfectly clear and that is that I know I already have fallen in love with you." You think I'm crazy don't you? "No not at all because I'm in love with you too and have been for a while." "What do you mean?" "I have been eyeing you of since you opened but I have never been able to get close enough to you to start anything with you." "Holy fuck so you mean I've been missing this for ages?" "Yes my sexual deviate?" By the way my name is Jasmine Johnson and I work for the local community bank, I'm the bank manager there." "I'm glad to meet you and fuck you Jasmine." "Like wise Mr Braxton Miles!" "You even know my name, how?" "Well for starters your name is written on the front of your establishment and two, your takings from the business come to me to deposit it into your business account!" "Jasmine you just said businesses, so you know about the other business?" "Of course, does it bother you or change anything about us as a couple?"

Oh hell no, do you think I would be here now if it did? "It actually titillates me and I think we can have some great fun and excellent sex there on occasions, don't you agree?" "Wholeheartedly, Jasmine, you're what I've been looking for my whole life. I knew the right person would be a sexual deviate like me and would love and cherish the same things that I do." I knew the right woman would be totally compatible and have a no holds barred approach for sexual gratification, with a high sexual appetite and passion and thirst for trying new things. "Well then Mr Hotshot I guess we really are a match made in heaven!" "You can say that again!" Just one more thing Jasmine and I hope you don't find this to forward and blunt, because I know we have only just known each other less than a week even though it feels like a lifetime, but would you move in with me into my house, soon to become, our house. ? "Why Mr Hot Shot you really are a spade and call it just how you see it!" Blunt though as you may be I would love to move in with you! "Then that is settled we will move you in on the weekend." I can't believe I no longer have to live like a single man out on the prowl.

Jasmine I'm so excited I have to ring Angel tomorrow and tell her, I'm in love and that I have found the one and only. You don't mind me telling her, do you? "Look if that makes you happy, and you love Angel then I know I will love her to!" I just hope she doesn't judge us for only knowing each other for a few days. "Trust me Angel and I go way back and she hasn't got a judgemental bone in her body, protective bones maybe but not judgemental!" I know for a fact that If I'm happy she will be equally happy for me, that's all she has ever wanted for me was to see me settle with one woman marry and have kids.

The next Braxton rings Angel on her mobile. "Hello my gorgeous business partner and friend, I haven't heard your voice or seen your since whenever, I was starting to think you may have been dead." "Ha funny Braxton you're so not the comedian." How you are and what can I do for you? How are the clubs holding up? "Firstly after talking to you I now know you're not dead and yes the clubs are doing famously." Angel you have no idea honey, that they have reached and they keep climbing. "That is so terrific I'm so happy both of our clubs have turned out profitable for us, it makes it all worthwhile in the end." "So am I dear, I can't believe how happy it has made me." Actually Angel the real reason I'm ringing you are for two reasons: the first being when you are expecting to return back to Auburn Creek and return back to work at the club." "Angel suddenly goes cold and doesn't know how to answer his question!" Responsively Zane takes the phone out of her possession, "hi Braxton" it's Zane! "Why hello Zane what's going on, now I know why Angel hasn't returned from or leave of absence or when she has plans to return to work? She is obviously having far too good a time with the Mr Dynamite himself! "Yes we are having a wonderful time together but that is not why she left and at the moment due to circumstances out of any of our control Angel will be out of action indefinitely!" "Zane what is going on? What is it you're not telling me?

"I can't talk about anything over the phone, so go and talk to Jett and Maddie and get the rundown from them." Braxton you have to promise on your life that you will not say anything to anyone about speaking to us or that Angel is here with me. "Okay Zane but you're certainly putting the wind up me!" "Everything will be okay if you just keep quiet." "Noted Zane and done!" "Thanks mate we both really appreciate it, now I will hand you back over to my beautiful one." "What was the other reason you called me asks Angel?"

"Well I couldn't wait any longer to tell you!" "Tell me what Braxton; hurry up the suspense is killing me?" "I can tell that being away still hasn't curbed your patience!" "Oh, please just get on with it and enough with the fucking sarcasm!" "Angel I'm in love! Real true love the way I had always imagined to be!" Her name is Jasmine Johnson and she is the bank Manager at our bank branch. "Do you know what the uncanny thing is?" "No how could I!" "She loves everything that I love and our compatibility is a hundred percent, and I met her at our club!" "Please don't tell me you met her at Knickerbox?

"No on the contrary it was at Nightlights, and I'm telling you Angel I have never been happier in my life than I am right now."

"Braxton if your happy and Jasmine makes you happy and if she is what you want then I'm absolutely over the moon for you both too." I can't wait to meet her! "I can't wait for you to meet her, Angel when you meet her you will see how down to earth she really is." "Jasmine, sounds just like what you have needed in your life for some time." I'm so very happy for you both and can't wait to come back down to meet her, but I really have to go now." "Fine, Angel I will let you go but just remember I will always cherish our friendship." With that the phone went dead and Braxton hung it up.

Bye the sounds of that phone call my beautiful one, it sounds like we're not the only ones that have found love. "Finally, Braxton is in love and has found someone that takes and accepts him for who he is, he is a unique kind of guy in a quirky kind of way, but that man really does have more heart than Midas has gold." I wonder if he will still need Knickerbox to satisfy his insatiable sexual hunger, or if Jasmine cuts it for him?

20

The Arrest

Storm Mason radios through to Blake Kristoff and explains to him that a couple of his patrol cops were patrolling and decided to stop and peek inside of the woman Rogue has been seen cavorting around town and bingo, he is in bed with her. "Great says Blake tell your guys to keep an eye on him until I get there!" get your guys to surround the house and stay waiting with the house surrounded. I will be there in ten minutes and I will send my men for backup. Within ten minutes Blake is at the scene and the whole house is surrounded. The men are all armed and wearing their protective gear and then Blake gives the order for the swat team to kick in the front door and in seconds Blake and the boys have Rogue in custody, pulling him out of bed and made him get dressed, they then hand cuff him and throw him in the back of the police paddy wagon. The boys get him back to the station and put him in the interview room. Blake and Storm start with the interrogation and question Rogue Tyler profusely. "Where the fuck is your step-brother?" we know what he has been going on, and we also know Robert has been using your auto shop to run his illegal dealings and that for whatever reason he had you over a barrel and because of that he is feeding you with his adulterated filthy money to keep you living your eccentric and exorbitant lifestyle. Also through our investigations we know you are broke and bankrupt. So start talking and tell us everything you know! Without the information we went, you're not going anywhere and we can't guarantee your safety or that you will be protected and looked after, and we can assure you, you will be getting locked up for a very long time. Now get on with it Rogue and start talking! No fucking bullshit from you!

"We'll All right!" I hadn't heard from my step brother in years, when dad and his ex-wife split up over twenty years ago his MOTHER Maureen Clarke took off with Robert, Patrick and Fiona, they were her kids and Robert was to my dad David Tyler. Robert was always a handful and out of control being the baby he was spoilt to the point of no return. Everything he wanted he got and when he was twelve he started a gang with the locals and they were wreaking havoc throughout the town that were living in. "Eventually his mother couldn't deal with him and as she had severed all ties with his dad and me we had no way of trying to help him. Finally when he was fifteen he went to a juvenile detention for manslaughter. They, the gang robbed an old pensioner who was getting money out of an ATM machine, the poor old bloke put up a fight so they beat the old bastard up that bad he never regained consciousness and the hospital and his family by his bedside turned his life support machine off. He was charged as an adult and was jailed and sentence to ten years with no parole and to serve his sentence in Pentridge Prison.

Although I never heard from him there was talk that he was dealing in drugs and also embezzling money through some internet scam and on top of that he was involved in credit fraud obtaining loans and credit cards under different aliases. "On the brink of the police closing in on him and ready to make an arrest, Robert got wind and fled. No one including myself had heard from him in years. About twelve months or so ago I put my accounts to the business to an accountant to find out why my bank account was dwindling. I knew I spent big but I also knew what money I had.

"After an investigation the accountant found that someone was hacking into my bank accounts and with them not being able to trace the offender they froze my accounts and all my credit; any money I wanted I had to go into the branch to withdraw it over the counter.

"About a month after, I came home from work late one afternoon and got the shock of my life to see Robert sitting on my couch watching television with a beer in his hand. It didn't take Robert long to let me know that he was the one hacking into my accounts and that he was pissed off because my accounts were frozen.

"Why did your accounts being frozen piss Robert off?" "Obviously he was using my account to run all his illegal dealings through and before long he had blown the lot trying to pay off his dealers and sharks."

Robert instructed me to have the freeze removed from my accounts and to keep my mouth shut, he also told me he would keep the funds coming as long as I kept my mouth shut and acted dumb.

Knowing what Robert was capable of I did as he said, and I thought he would eventually move on. Here we are a year later and he is still here leeching of me and dragging me around likes a cyclone dragging the roof of a house! I stayed away from him more and more and longer and longer at the club. Drinking myself into oblivion and gambling and screwing all the local sheila's that I could pick up.

I later met Maryanne James, for who it was her house that you cops picked me up from, and in no time at all we fell in love. I told Maryanne what was happening and that I wanted Robert out of my life and she advised me to go to the cops. I knew though that, that definitely wasn't a good idea and definitely not a safe idea for both of us.

After a while I got an idea to take the books to Fergusson's Accounting and knowing about Wade and Angel's savvy reputations and competence I knew they would pick up the discrepancies. For the first time in a year I felt like it was soon finally going to be over and that they would track it all back to Robert.

"So you're telling us you wanted this all out in the open and your step-brother caught?" "I'm absolutely telling you this is the case!" "Do you know where he is now, hiding out?" "I'm not positive but I know he has an old shack left to him from his mother down by the river somewhere basically covered around swamp!" "Can you take us there?" "I can but I'm not; I'm telling you this is not an option if he saw me or knew I was telling you he would kill me or have me killed!" "Can you at least give us instructions and directions?" "I'm prepared to do that!"

"Okay I will bring Maryanne in here and we will still protect both of you, and Rogue thanks for cooperating with us!" Blake picks up Maryanne and instructs her to grab a bag of clothes and necessities that she thinks they will need and takes her to the police protection house at the back of the station.

"Storm I need to contact Zane immediately and meanwhile you need to get your men to surround Robert's shack." I will set my team up ready also; we do need to get on top of this now in case he escapes again."

Blake and storm map out the directions and follow the instructions Rogue has given them and then the teams disembark and take off to get ready and get into position and get ready for the raid.

"Hi Zane It's me Blake?" "Hi Blake you better have been ringing me with fucking good news?" "I'm the messenger bearing you good news!" "Blake what have you got for me?" "We have Rogue Tyler in custody and his girlfriend Maryanne James held at our protection house!" You were right Rogue was forced and blackmailed into helping Robert. Scared stiff he refused to take us to show where his dumpy shabby shack is he thinks he will be hiding out in.

I have set all the teams in motion and they have the shack surrounded. Storm and I are on our way down there now to lead the raid. "We have him Zane; he will be in custody and will make sure he never gets released from prison!" Auburn Creek, Angel, Wade and his family can all come back here and get back to living a normal life again. "Fucking great news get that bastard and then I will see him at headquarters, that bastard is going to pay!" now get on with it. "Fuck this up and you will all have to deal with me." "I assure you Zane we won't mess this up, we will get him!" I have to go now; I will ring you when we have that son of a bitch in our custody. "Great keep me updated!"

An hour later everyone is in place all loaded with weapons and their protective clothing including bullet proof vests on, and then Blake and some of the team kick in the front door, and Storm and the team smash in the back door. They find the Robert Mullins trying to climb up into the manhole but they have all ambushed him and he has nowhere to go. Knowing he is done for he puts his hands up above his hands and surrenders. Blake hand cuffs him and the swat team drag him outside and put him in the paddy wagon.

"Good work Blake you and the boys got him!" "Great job well, done!"

"Thanks Storm but we all did it." Now we get him to the station, read him his rights and charge him. Then we can get him sent to Police Headquarters to await trial. This time he won't see the light of day ever!

Robert arrives at the police station; Storm reads out the list of charges, reads Robert his rights, takes his statement makes him read it and then signs it. Storm asks Robert if he pleads guilty. Robert knows he can't get out of this the evidence is definitely stacked up against him so he pleads guilty and reads and signs the statement.

Blake and his security team arrange and organise to fly him to Sydney where he will be remanded to appear in court awaiting his sentencing.

The police and Blake aboard the plane with Robert in hand and ankle cuffs and the plane take off for the twenty five minute flight to Sydney Airport.

"Hi Zane its Blake, I have great news, we've got him and were on the plane with him to headquarters as we speak!" "What is your arrival time?" "We are due in at ten thirty, gives us forty minutes with the traffic and meet us at HQ at say around eleven thirty am!" "Leave the charges and him to me; I'm going to make that worthless bastard pay!"

Eleven thirty and Zane find himself face to face with the bastard that kept Angel and Wade undercover for months. His temper is inflating and the fire and rage in his eyes are raging like a bull to a red rag. Zane jumps up and grabs Robert around the throat, "I'm going to kill you, you bastard no one threatens my girlfriend or people close or associated with." The more Zane thought about Robert the more his grip tightened around his throat.

Robert was turning bright red and his lips were turning blue, he was starting to cough and gasp for breath, begging Zane to leave him alone, and just at that moment Blake and their team pulled Zane off him and pushed him outside.

"Zane I know how you feel and believe me if I thought we could kill him I would let you, but you know as well as I do killing him will affect your life for ever." Your life with that sexy hot woman of yours would be no more.

"Your right I do need to calm down and I need to see him locked away for life." "I guarantee you Zane Robert Mullins will never be around to cause trouble for Angel, Wade or anyone else again." So why don't you go back to that beautiful misses or yours and break the good news to her?

21

Their Successes

One month later the jury comes back to the court with a verdict "Guilty" and the court room erupts, the judge hands down his sentence, Robert Mullins you have been found guilty on all charges so I'm ordering you to serve them all concurrently, I'm awarding you the maximum I'm allowed other believe me you would never be getting out and that is if you do anyway, I sentence you to thirty five years with a non-parole period and no intention for an appeal. Sheriff takes him away please?

Rogue Tyler was let off with a two year good behaviour bond and ordered to attend rehab for his alcohol substance, he has now been able to live free from the threats and fear that had put the wind up him from his step-brother with his soon to be wife Maryanne James who has put Rogue on a new path and helped him become a better man, a much happier man who has finally found contentment in his life.

Braxton and Angel are relishing in their glory of the success of not one but both their businesses. In the short months since the opening of Knickerbox both businesses have put them in the millionaires, category.

Finally all of Braxton's dreams have come true through his and Angel's brilliant and genius business acumen, he is finally sitting on millionaire's row.

Just a week or so ago he went and bought himself a silver/ grey Lamborghini and Jasmine a red Porsche. They're both building a two-storey mansion right on the lake front at the main entrance on Highway three as you come into Auburn Creek, their balcony has amazing views; they have a full three hundred and sixty degree view overlooking the entire sites of Auburn Grove. Braxton has bought himself a yacht for which he has moored with the upper class yachtsmen at the local marina. Both Braxton and Jasmine are making plans to sail around the world in their yacht.

Jett Marks has received accolades for the magnificent Mega Plex Plaza that is now completed and drawing in big crowds, and through his skill and the love of his design he is drawing in offers from all over the country.

The council did a podium presentation to mark the achievements of Jett Marks work and design at the opening presentation of the Mega Plaza and gave Jett the honours of cutting the ribbons.

Jett and his working gang all received accolades, praise and an award each for the group effort that helped put the Mega Plaza together.

Wade and his family have since returned to Auburn Creek but after the ordeal they as a whole family were put through have put Wade Fergusson Accounting up for sale after approaching Angel with the first offer to buy him out so they can return to their new life they had man on The North Shore an affluent suburb in the north of Sydney. Angel however had agreed to stay on for the whole running of the business until the new owners that are buying Wade out start out with their new business.

Jett and Maddie's relationship keeps getting stronger by the day and both tell everyone they fall in love more every day. They have both finally moved into their dream home built by Jett and designed by Maddie only it is more of a palace than a luxury house. They both spend most of their spend time working out and training at the gym, making love or sitting out under their big enclosed gabled veranda admiring the workmanship and the finished product.

Storm Mason is still leading the charge at the local police station but will hand the reins over to the next senior in line at the Christmas breakup end of year celebrations. Storm wants to retire so he can relax and spend more quality time with his wife, children and grandchildren. He so desperately wants to watch his grandchildren grow up and be involved in their lives which are something through his dedication and career in the police force never got to watch his own children grow up. He missed valuable moments in their lives and doesn't want to make the same regrets as he with his children. Jane his wife and he also want to take time out to travel to some Australian and overseas destinations.

Well Braxton and Jasmine are just so in love it is actually quite sickening, no one thought Braxton could settle down with just one woman and be so totally smitten and in love with just the one as he is with Jasmine. A match made in heaven says the locals in the town. Angel herself his struck with the notion of how he can settle just with Jasmine and walk away from his bizarre sex style, and his voracious sexual appetite. Obviously Jasmine offers him all that and more, not that Angel isn't happy for him because her best buddy has finally found true love and is happy and devoted to his woman. Braxton and Angel still own the businesses and he still runs the both businesses but now doesn't need Knickerbox to release some of his sexual needs and fantasies.

Angel and Zane get more in love with each other every day if that is possible and don't like to be apart, and although Angel isn't aware Zane has some very big plans for the both of them and an announcement to everyone that they are involved with. She no longer works at any of her businesses she takes her earnings from it on a weekly basis. Due to most of Zane's work load being in the city they are both in the process of tying off their lose ends and making their new life at their retreat in Sydney and Zane wants Angel to be available to accompany him on as many work trips as she can possibly do with him. They hate to spend even a minute apart from each other, now that is real love. They are both concentrating on the hopeful idea of Angel being pregnant and the hope and joy for them both to become parents in the very near future.

22

Two Weddings and an Engagement

Six months after their ordeal everyone's lives are finally back to a normal life with lots of working, loving and sex. Zane is working on a case in Sydney and this time Angel opted to stay behind in Auburn Creek and not to accompany him, as she is frantically working and catching up on her workload in readiness for the owners with the new buy out from Wade Fergusson. There are things that she has needed to do and other things that needed to be finished from co-workers also before the big day. Although Angel spent a great number of years working at Wade Fergusson Accounting and even being promoted to Manager she opted to not stay on with the new owners, because she wants to spend her time in Sydney with Zane and be free with no ties to accompany Zane on his work trips when it permits her to go. It has been three weeks since they have last seen each other which is the longest time they have been apart since the threats made against her from Robert Mullins when Zane took her under wing to protect her from him. each day they are apart the harder it keeps getting for them both, the harder Angel finds it to concentrate, and the more frustrated, hornier and sexier she gets. For this super couple who would average having sex a minimum of three times per day not even having it at least once a day is taking its toll on both of them.

Angel knows her man better than he or anyone else knows him she can imagine by how frustrated, lonely and horny she is feeling, how much her Mr Dynamite would be suffering. His feelings would be that of impatience, torment, fury and loneliness and like her would be doing the final countdown to when they can both be back in each other's arms and their bed. She also knows that that when he does return back to her their sexual passion, their lovemaking, their drive and the intensity that only they share will be made up for lost time.

With the thoughts of what is to come and in store for her has made her so moist and wet and impatient for the waiting for his return, she knows she must stay calm and focus on the image she is picturing in her mind of what Zane will do to her when he returns.

Although she is missing Zane impeccably she can't believe how fast the past three weeks have just flown, she has been so busy getting her workload done in order for the takeover with the new owners. Angel also wants to set their house for a romantic setting for Zane's return home. Angel spent a whole day looking through her sexy lingerie she brought during her summer when Zane had walked away from her and left her behind. Her idea is to be laying on the lounge in her lingerie when Zane walks through their door. "Oh my god" I've seen stars just visualising this picture in my mind knowing what was going to happen to her the moment Zane lays eyes on her in her lingerie. Here is the picture for you all to visualise. (Zane walks through the door sees Angel on the couch in her lingerie, {something's she knows he just can't refuse} an instant erection, he rips his clothes off and in no time he is on her pleasuring her sending her to the brink of carnal pleasure as only her Mr Dynamite can). Yes alright you all get the picture! Angel has aromatic candles set all around the house, starting at the front door through the hall way and the lounge/ living area and finishing in their bedroom. They are setting of some rich succulent smells and Angel is also hoping they are going to work as an aphrodisiac to spice up the mood.

Jett and Maddie are returning in a couple of days after a cruise around the Pacific Islands, it's been Jett's first holiday in many years and a definitely much needed admits Angel. Jett wanted to share a romantic holiday with his long-time girlfriend and Angel's best friend Maddie Carter. Angel can only imagine how much of a princess Jett has made of her, getting her anything she wanted and spoiling her like Crazy.

Braxton and Jasmine (well Angel has not heard from them in ages) so expects they are still on the cloud of love and enjoying each other's company and knowing Braxton probably won't have jasmine out of their bed for very long either.

Storm his wife Christine and family are relishing in his retirement and catching up on long lost family time. Storm is also enjoying the weekly game of golf and has taken a special shine in taking his grandchildren out fishing, going to the playground, kicking the ball around, playing soccer or just for enjoyable walks through the parks. Every week they share a family dinner or a BBQ.

Wade and his family and his very patient wife Julie have bought a small family business in the North Shore suburbs of Sydney after having made their big move from quiet sleepy hollow Auburn Creek to the hustle and bustle and very fast life in Sydney but one they all believe was in need of changing for the better. Surprisingly they have all adapted exceptionally well to their new city life. A complete new start for Wade and his family and a complete and whole new career path and one that the whole family can work at and receive the benefits that will come with the business. After Wade's thirty plus years as an accountant with his own accountancy firm Wade assured Angel that although he will miss his job and his lifestyle he will definitely not have any regrets with his new way of life and was definitely his time to move on in his life for a whole new direction and meaning to his life.

Although her job and role at Wade Fergusson was a great job and a fantastic opportunity Angel also has no regrets in moving forward with the new stage in her life, it is time to move forward start a new chapter for her future and leave her past behind her. Hopefully she can leave all traces from her past life and make and enjoy to the maximum and love life to its fullest with the only love of her life her Mr Dynamite, Zane Channing. Nothing could be more satisfying and rewarding and completed than spending the rest of her life with the most incredible loving sensual man she has ever known.

Angel's task of setting the romantic scene is complete she goes and soaks in a luxurious, foaming bubble bath and relaxes for a time. An hour later she has done her hair and fitted her lingerie, she has chosen a complete set in the most gorgeous alluring and sensual deep purple. Her lingerie consists of a baby doll open front tie top, a pair of matching crotch less panties, fish net stockings in black with matching purple garters around the tops of her thighs, a dark purple garter tied tightly at the front with lace, a very teeny bra, underneath her baby doll top, and to top off her outfit she has straightened her hair because that is how her man loves her hair long and straight, so decides to give it just that bit of oomph by putting some purple ribbons in her hair.

Angel is patiently waiting because she knows at any moment Zane will be walking through the front door, she hears the car pull up and she is in her waiting position on the lounge holding a glass of wine, she is trembling and shaking, anxious and tense, but feeling very sexy and horny. Angel knows this plan is a sure fire wins and that she can't possibly lose. In no time at all Zane comes through the front door, the lights are off and the candles are burning brightly and Zane walks into the entrance way and he is mesmerized, gobsmacked, in awe, star stuck he can't believe what he is seeing let alone what he has come home too. Zane can feel his manhood rise straight to attention, and he has this feeling he is in for a great time and possibly one of the best times in all his life. "Angel where are you he calls out?" "I'm in the lounge room baby! "he throws his bag on the side table and walks close to the lounge and spots his beautiful one all setup in her glorious, sexy lingerie and in no time at all Zane has stripped totally naked and he is all over Angel, kissing and tonguing her, beautifully his hands are rubbing her neck, back, down her legs and kissing and nibbling at her ear-lobes and neck at the same time. Angel is ecstatic to have her man home right where he needs to be with her and back in her arms. She runs her fingers through his hair and outlines his face with the tips of her fingers and kisses him around his face, neck and kisses his lips passionately and they both put their tongues in each other's mouths, tonguing and kissing so intensely.

Zane's cock has just got that hard and erect it is sitting against Angel's leg; she can feel the length and girth that she has so craved over the past few weeks. Zane lays Angel down flat and put her legs over his shoulders and in seconds has buried head at her triangular mound he has come to love nearly as much as he loves her. He can already smell the scent from her sex which has already nearly sent him over the edge, sticks his tongue in her pussy and hits her clitoris with the tip of his tongue. Angel quivers, the intensity is so strong, he already has her squirming and squealing, moaning, shrieking with pleasure each tongue longer, stronger more intense than the one before. She pleads for Zane to stop, but he is relentless, he puts two fingers inside her at the same time; she screams with pain, pleasure, fulfilment. Angel is numb, so sensitive and satisfied but not wanting him to stop. She pushes Zane out of her and down on his back and in no time at all she is kissing him and licking him all down his body sending the most sensational, tingling he has ever endured, then she made her move, straight for his erect rod sucking him hungrily like it was going to be her last feed ever.

Zane can't believe how much hunger she has, how much ferocity; she is giving him pure carnal sexual lust. Angel has Zane on the verge as she licks his entire shaft, takes him deep, deeper than she has ever taken him before, he is euphoric, dazed, unbelievably sexual and trying his dam nest to hold back his release. Angel travels down his shaft playing with his balls and sucking them, draining his love juice from his gorgeous love sacks, she nibbles at the head of his cock sucking along the veins, which are sending his blood flow stronger in making his erection even more engorged.

Zane can feel the moisture from her sex and her scent is sending him his favourite odour; the most aromatic scent he ever smells besides his beautiful one.

Angel stop and let me put my cock inside your tight pussy, I can't hold my juice any longer, for once my beautiful I'm begging and pleading for you to stop. "Oh my god Angel I have to go away more often and leave you behind, your relentless tonight." I have never experienced anything like this before in my entire life and I'm not going to be able to hold back any longer and I really need to feel your sweet, tight pussy around my big fucking seriously horny cock.

Angel lays on her back and he holds her legs above her and flips them over his shoulders and in no time at all he is thrusting his long man rod deep into her pussy, harder and deeper he is riding her like there is no tomorrow! Angel attempts to strip her lingerie off. "Stop!" leave them on please my beautiful one, they have really gotten me off tonight watching and seeing you in those beautiful clothes and I'm happy to keep on fucking you through these crotch less panties, your pussy with my cock pumping in it looks sensational, your lobes hitting against the edge of your panties and they are so moist and saturated with your wetness from your love box.

Angel is matching Zane thrust for thrust taking him so deep that he can feel his royalties loading inside him and Angel can feel him pulsating and throbbing inside her and that's all she needs to send her to an erotic, forceful climatic eruption, that's it baby you've done me proud tonight, you've done it for me now I'm going to shoot my load deep inside your pussy. They're both thrashing about and moving, writhing, they have both just gone through their most climatic and eruptive orgasm to date. They tidy themselves up and cuddle and embrace each other on the couch.

Zane asks Angel about her time while he was away and how the buyout from Fergusson's went? Both exchanged small talk catching up with the past couple of weeks of being apart.

Zane can I cook you a delicious meal for dinner? "Um, No!" I thought I would think ahead I have already made dinner reservations at your favourite restaurant, so we had both better get ready our reservations are made for seven pm.

"Great do you want to have a shower with me?" "My beautiful one, just try to keep me out while you're in there!" Zane and Angel both shower together lathering up and soaping up the loofah to wash each other and they clean each other from head to toe, climb out and Zane dries every inch of Angel's body." My turn to dry you now Mr Dynamite." No, you need the extra time to get ready, so hurry up we have dinner to go to. Well Mr bossy britches aye captain. "Honestly Angel, you're *incorrigible!*" "I know but you love me!" "You've got that right, but love is an understatement." "Aw you're such a soft touch!"

At seven pm, they are seated at the restaurant and they both ordered from the menus. The waiter recommended Cabernet Sauvignon with their main and both agreed the choice was perfect. Angel is impatiently tapping her fingers on the table and Zane puts his hands on hers to stop her annoying tapping. "Angel my beautiful one, whatever is wrong with you tonight?" "I'm starving and the meal seems to be taking forever!" Then within a second of her speaking, two guitar playing singers come at their table serenading them, Whitney Huston hit "I will always love you." At the same time the waiter brings out their main course, he takes the lids of each meal and right in front of Angel positioned perfectly on her plate is a four carat diamond and yellow gold wedding ring. "Zane what is this for, you have already bought me my engagement ring," "No my beautiful one the first one was our practice run, this is the real deal." Before Angel can even think Zane his down on one knee on the side of her and asks Angel to marry him. "Will you please do the honour in marrying me and becoming my wife?" Although red with embarrassment and tears of joy running down her cheeks she manages to get out her answer. "Yes Zane of course I will marry you!" Everyone in the restaurant is cheering and clapping and congratulations are coming from everywhere. Zane has Angel embraced in his arms as they kiss passionately and before the embrace is over a lady delivers a hundred red roses to Angel at the table with a big sign attached saying (Angel I love you). Now that you have accepted my proposal my beautiful please pick a date? "What right here, right now?" "I haven't got a calendar?" I have my diary on me. "Trust you to think of everything!" "Well I definitely want the warmer weather, so maybe November or December?" "December was my choice and I thought maybe a Christmas wedding, say Saturday the twenty fourth of December!" That is so perfect, the twenty fourth it is! I don't want a big wedding Zane just an intimate wedding with our closest family and friends. "Are you sure? Because, you know money is no object?" do you want to invite your folks? "Absolutely not, Zane please don't go there and spoil this evening?" "Alright leave it at that!" "Do you want to invite your family?" "Same as you babe, let's leave that one well alone!" "Zane, would you mind if I asked Wade to give me away?

He is the closest thing to a real father figure that Jett and I have ever really had and who counts? "Baby you don't have to ask me that, you can have whoever you want?" "Now would you mind if I asked Jett to be my groomsman?" "I and I know Jett would be privileged." "You know that Maddie would be my maid of honour; but I think I will ask Jasmine to be my bridesmaid! "And my beautiful one I'm going to ask Blake to be my best man." "Simply Perfect!" I couldn't be happier than I am at this time.

Zane do you know how much I love you? "Angel I know how much you love me because I love you more than life itself, you complete me, well almost all I need is our children and I want to start working on them right away."

The next morning Angel calls up Jett, Wade, Braxton, Blake and Storm and their respective partners and invites them all around for cocktails and nibbles.

Seven thirty everyone has arrived and are all gathered and mingling, drinking beer and cocktails and nibbling on cocktail food.

Zane pulls Angel to him and asks everyone for their undivided attention. Everyone Angel and I got you all here to make an announcement. I proposed to Angel and she luckily has accepted my proposal.

Well it's about fucking time you two got your shit together it is well over due, were just some of the comments being thrown around the room. They were both smothered with kisses on the cheeks, handshakes and hugs from their guests.

Then Jet stands up to make a speech and with him embracing Maddie they announce, "well everyone you all know by now Maddie and I have just returned from our cruise and while we were away I too proposed to my long-time lover and best friend Madison Carter and she has also agreed to be my wife!" The whole room stood in shock staring at everyone else's reactions and waiting to see who was going to speak or act first. Suddenly Angel breaks the silence code, and congratulates her brother and her best friend. "I'm so happy for you both I couldn't be happier." I haven't lost a brother I have gained a sister. Everyone then starts hugging, kissing and congratulating them also.

Maddie is so ecstatic and starts showing off her blue topaz and diamond on white gold two carat diamond engagement ring. "Oh no look Jett, Angel's ring is much bigger than mine!" "That is okay Maddie yours suits you and that one is your style." "Jett your right and this doesn't change how much I love you and how excited I is to be your wife." Maddie suggests that seems both couples have announced their engagements that maybe it they should hold a double wedding. The look on Angel and Zane's face said it all, it was completely obvious that they did not want to share their event with Jett and Maddie.

Angel was stammering, trying to find the words she wanted but for the first time Angel was actually speechless, so Zane stepped up to come to Angel's defence and explained "we are very happy for you both, as we know you are for us, but I don't want the limelight taken of my beautiful one on her day, and Maddie I'm sure you would agree that you want your wedding day to be all about you."

With that statement everyone was in agreement. "Angel and myself, have both agreed we would like a Christmas wedding and have set Saturday the twenty fourth of December as our wedding day, so while we are on the subject I would like to ask Blake if he would do me the honour of being my best man and Jett if you would be my groomsman." Both were delighted in the privilege and couldn't accept quickly enough. Then Angel steps up and asks "Maddie would you please be my maid of honour?" "God girl I thought you would never ask; of course?" "Jasmine I would be thrilled if you would be my bridesmaid?" "I couldn't possibly find a refusal there, thanks so much Angel for considering me!" "Too finish off I have one more request and that is, Wade you're the only father figure and the only one that has been around to help Jett and I settle into Auburn Grove at such a young age, you took us both under your wing and gave me the offer of a lifetime, so I was wondering if you would please give me away?" "Angel I don't know what to say only that this would have to be one of the proudest moments in my life and I would be honoured to step up and give you away." With that Angel, Wade and his wife wipe the tears from their cheeks and have a long drawn out hug.

The group all ask about Jett and Maddie's wedding date and they are proud to announce that they will wed on New Year's Eve. They also put out their wedding party invites and they are all happy proud to be part of their momentous occasion. The rest of the guests are also clearly happy and thrilled with the news.

Congratulations all around, and Zane asks everyone to raise a toast to the announcements which have come through for the respective proposals. Now with everyone happy, drinking beers, and wines, and cocktails and nibbling on food and just enjoying the presence of everyone's company, Braxton stands to the front and asks everyone for their attention too? Jasmine is locked tightly in Braxton's arms and he speaks. "I must tell you all that you Angel and Zane and Jett and Maddie have tonight certainly knocked the wind out of me because both Jasmine and I also announced our engagement and we also wanted to share and announce it to you all tonight as well. Jasmine has made me the happiest man in the world and the happiest I could ever be and "yes I know, I bet most of your thought I would never settle down with one woman, but as you would all be aware of love not only makes you do stupid things it makes you change your views on life, so thanks everyone for all your love and support and in particular for allowing Jasmine into our own unique little circle."

Zane stands to the front and sends out the congratulations once again to Braxton and his beautiful fiancé, Jasmine. "Everyone please raise your glasses one final time for a toast to the engagement announcement of one Braxton Miles and the beautiful Jasmine Johnson.

The big night finally came to end and Zane commented to Angel, "What a night my beautiful one, two weddings and an engagement!" "I know one thing Mr Dynamite it has definitely been one incredible year for romances!" With that they both turned in for the night.

23

The Announcement

One month later Zane and Angel have returned from their around the world honeymoon and living in their Sydney retreat and Angel is just glowing. Zane you completed me and made me the happiest woman in the world. "Angel I can't express to you in enough words how much you mean to me, how much I love you and how you also complete me. I love you more everyday day and love you to the entire universe, moon and stars and back.

Zane we need to contact the others and let them know we're home and see how Jett and Maddie went on their honeymoon and how Braxton and Jasmine have held up since their engagement. "Sounds like a good idea my beautiful one, do you want to invite them over here or get them to meet us somewhere?" "I'll ring them all and ask them and see what they say!" "Angel it's a jolly, great idea!"

Angel waits for Zane to go into his study to check his in box and messages, so she quickly rings Maddie and asks her to help her with a favour and a surprise. "Why of course, we will drive to the city tonight and meet at your place; I'll tell the girls there coming out with us and the boys that they are going with Zane!" "Please don't let on about the secret to anyone and I will leave the inviting up to you and see you all tonight!" The next morning Angel awakes and is happy and excited to get her plans underway to help her prepare for the surprise she has in store for her Mr Dynamite.

That afternoon the whole gang arrives and the boys head down to the local pub for drinks, and the girls all pile into Angel's new BMW four wheel drive Zane bought her for a wedding present. The boys pile into Jett's black land cruiser and take off to the pub.

Angel leads the girls into the shops and buys what she wants and everything she thinks she will need, and they all help her load it into the car. "My god Angel this is an overload if there ever was one, says Jasmine and then all the girls giggle amongst themselves."

Fifteen minutes later they arrived back at the house and had everything unloaded and taken up the stairs to the second bedroom. Angel called for their maintenance man, the gardened and the maid to help her and the girls get everything set up and put together before the guys got home. An hour and a half later everything is set up and put in place. "Great job everyone, now we just wait for the boys to bring Angel's man back home to her."

The girl's pops the champagne bottles but Angel settled on water and in no time at all the boys are walking through the front door. "Hi guys your back, how was the pub?" Zane immediately walks over to his woman and smothers her with passionate kisses and hugs. "Did you miss me my beautiful one?" "More Mr Dynamite than you would ever know?" The guys can't get over the look on the girls faces and all notice they are acting strange 'like the cat that ate the canary'. Jett comes forward, brash and high and mighty and spurts out, 'you girls are all up to something'. What have you done or what are you hiding? Yes come clean, says the other guys! "We don' know what you're talking about says Maddie with a sense of cheekiness about her."

Zane can I get you to follow me for a moment please? I have something to show you! "Zane's eyebrows rise and his eyes roll and reply your wish baby is my command." "Why? Zane! Please we have company!" "I'm sure our visitors won't mind us leaving them for a while." "Oh my god Mr Dynamite, you really are a horny beast!" With that comment everyone laughs! Zane follows Angel into the second bedroom, he stares, mute, unable to take it all in, unable to speak and then Angel finally breaks the silence and asks Zane what he thinks? "It's a nursery, but why?" "My baby, are you?" "Yes my man I'm pregnant with your baby, um sorry our baby." He screams out and grabs Angel, holds her up in the above his head and spins her around. He then realises that everyone is gathered around them in the room. Zane can't stop the tears running down his cheeks, oh my beautiful one you have made me the happiest man in the world and now I really and truly am complete, and I can't believe we're going to be parents.

The gang are all cheering and clapping and the congratulations are all flowing, while Zane and Angel embraced and kissed passionately, and Zane had her held tightly in his embrace and never wanted to let her go again.

The End

Printed in the United States
By Bookmasters